Chivalry
James Branch Cabell

MINT EDITIONS

Chivalry was first published in 1909.

This edition published by Mint Editions 2020.

ISBN 9781513267609 | E-ISBN 9781513272603

Published by Mint Editions®

MINT
EDITIONS

minteditionbooks.com

Publishing Director: Jennifer Newens
Design & Production: Rachel Lopez Metzger
Typesetting: Westchester Publishing Services

Contents

Chivalry

The Prologue

À sa Dame

I nasmuch as it was by your command, illustrious and exalted lady, that I have gathered together these stories to form the present little book, you should the less readily suppose I have presumed to dedicate to your Serenity this trivial offering because of my esteeming it to be not undeserving of your acceptance. The truth is otherwise; and your postulant now approaches as one not spurred toward you by vainglory but rather by plain equity, and simply in acknowledgment of the fact that he who seeks to write of noble ladies must necessarily implore at outset the patronage of her who is the light and mainstay of our age. In fine, I humbly bring my book to you as Phidyle approached another and less sacred shrine, *farre pio et salente mica*, and lay before you this my valueless mean tribute not as appropriate to you but as the best I have to offer.

It is a little book wherein I treat of divers queens and of their love-business; and with necessitated candor I concede my chosen field to have been harvested, and even scrupulously gleaned, by many writers of innumerable conditions. Since Dares Phrygius wrote of Queen Heleine and Virgil (that shrewd necromancer) of Queen Dido, a preponderating mass of clerks, in casting about for high and serious matter, have chosen, as though it were by common instinct, to dilate upon the amours of royal women. Even in romance we scribblers must contrive it so that the fair Nicolette shall be discovered in the end to be no less than the King's daughter of Carthage, and that Sir Doon of Mayence shall never sink in his love-affairs beneath the degree of a Saracen princess; and we are backed in this old procedure not only by the authority of Aristotle but, oddly enough, by that of reason as well.

Kings have their policies and wars wherewith to drug each appetite. But their consorts are denied these makeshifts; and love may rationally be defined as the pivot of each normal woman's life, and in consequence as the arbiter of that ensuing life which is eternal. Because—as of old Horatius Flaccus demanded, though not, to speak the truth, of any woman,—

Quo fugis? ah demons! nulla est fuga, tu licet usque
Ad Tanaim fugias, usque sequetur amor.

And a dairymaid, let us say, may love whom she will, and nobody else be a penny the worse for her mistaking of the preferable nail whereon to hang her affections; whereas with a queen this choice is more portentous. She plays the game of life upon a loftier table, ruthlessly illuminated, and stakes by her least movement a tall pile of counters, some of which are, of necessity, the lives and happiness of persons whom she knows not, unless it be by vague report. Grandeur sells itself at this hard price, and at no other. A queen must always play, in fine, as the vicar of destiny, free to choose but very certainly compelled to justify that choice in the ensuing action; as is strikingly manifested by the authentic histories of Brunhalt, and of Guenevere, and of swart Cleopatra, and of many others that were born to the barbaric queenhoods of a now extinct and dusty time.

For royal persons are (I take it) the immediate and the responsible stewards of Heaven; and since the nature of each man is like a troubled stream, now muddied and now clear, their prayer must ever be, *Defenda me, Dios, de me*! Yes, of exalted people, and even of their near associates, life, because it aims more high than the aforementioned Aristotle, demands upon occasion a more great catharsis which would purge any audience of unmanliness, through pity and through terror, because, by a quaint paradox, the players have been purged of all humanity. For in that aweful moment would Destiny have thrust her sceptre into the hands of a human being and Chance would have exalted a human being into usurpal of her chair. These two—with what immortal chucklings one may facilely imagine—would then have left the weakling thus enthroned, free to direct the pregnant outcome, free to choose, and free to steer the conjuration either in the fashion of Friar Bacon or of his man, but with no intermediate course unbarred. *Now prove thyself!* saith Destiny; and Chance appends: *Now prove thyself to be at bottom a god or else a beast, and now eternally abide that choice. And now* (O crowning irony!) *we may not tell thee clearly by which choice thou mayst prove either*.

It is of ten such moments that I treat within this little book.

You alone, I think, of all persons living have learned, as you have settled by so many instances, to rise above mortality in such a testing, and unfailingly to merit by your conduct the plaudits and the adoration of our otherwise dissentient world. You have sat often in this same high chair of Chance; and in so doing have both graced and hallowed it. Yet I forbear to speak of this, simply because I dare not seem to couple your well-known perfection with any imperfect encomium.

Therefore to you, madame—most excellent and noble lady,
to whom I love to owe both loyalty and love—
I dedicate this little book.

I

The Story of the Sestina

In this place we have to do with the opening tale of the Dizain of Queens. I abridge, as afterward, at discretion; and an initial account of the Barons' War, among other superfluities, I amputate as more remarkable for veracity than interest. The result, we will agree at outset, is that to the Norman cleric appertains whatever these tales may have of merit, whereas what you find distasteful in them you must impute to my delinquencies in skill rather than in volition.

Within the half-hour after de Giars' death (here one overtakes Nicolas mid-course in narrative) Dame Alianora thus stood alone in the corridor of a strange house. Beyond the arras the steward and his lord were at irritable converse.

First, "If the woman be hungry," spoke a high and peevish voice, "feed her. If she need money, give it to her. But do not annoy me."

"This woman demands to see the master of the house," the steward then retorted.

"O incredible Boeotian, inform her that the master of the house has no time to waste upon vagabonds who select the middle of the night as an eligible time to pop out of nowhere. Why did you not do so in the beginning, you dolt?" He got for answer only a deferential cough, and very shortly continued: "This is remarkably vexatious. *Vox et praeterea nihil*,—which signifies, Yeck, that to converse with women is always delightful. Admit her." This was done, and Dame Alianora came into an apartment littered with papers, where a neat and shrivelled gentleman of fifty-odd sat at a desk and scowled.

He presently said, "You may go, Yeck." He had risen, the magisterial attitude with which he had awaited her advent cast aside. "O God!" he said; "you, madame!" His thin hands, scholarly hands, were plucking at the air.

Dame Alianora had paused, greatly astonished, and there was an interval before she said, "I do not recognize you, messire."

"And yet, madame, I recall very clearly that some thirty years ago Count Berenger, then reigning in Provence, had about his court four daughters, each one of whom was afterward wedded to a king. First,

Margaret, the eldest, now regnant in France; then Alianora, the second and most beautiful of these daughters, whom troubadours hymned as La Belle. She was married a long while ago, madame, to the King of England, Lord Henry, third of that name to reign in these islands."

Dame Alianora's eyes were narrowing. "There is something in your voice," she said, "which I recall."

He answered: "Madame and Queen, that is very likely, for it is a voice which sang a deal in Provence when both of us were younger. I concede with the Roman that I have somewhat deteriorated since the reign of good Cynara. Yet have you quite forgotten the Englishman who made so many songs of you? They called him Osmund Heleigh."

"He made the Sestina of Spring which my father envied," the Queen said; and then, with a new eagerness: "Messire, can it be that you are Osmund Heleigh?" He shrugged assent. She looked at him for a long time, rather sadly, and afterward demanded if he were the King's man or of the barons' party. The nervous hands were raised in deprecation.

"I have no politics," he began, and altered it, gallantly enough, to, "I am the Queen's man, madame."

"Then aid me, Osmund," she said; and he answered with a gravity which singularly became him:

"You have reason to understand that to my fullest power I will aid you."

"You know that at Lewes these swine overcame us." He nodded assent. "And now they hold the King my husband captive at Kenilworth. I am content that he remain there, for he is of all the King's enemies the most dangerous. But, at Wallingford, Leicester has imprisoned my son, Prince Edward. The Prince must be freed, my Osmund. Warren de Basingbourne commands what is left of the royal army, now entrenched at Bristol, and it is he who must liberate him. Get me to Bristol, then. Afterward we will take Wallingford." The Queen issued these orders in cheery, practical fashion, and did not admit opposition into the account, for she was a capable woman.

"But you, madame?" he stammered. "You came alone?"

"I come from France, where I have been entreating—and vainly entreating—succor from yet another monkish king, the pious Lewis of that realm. Eh, what is God about when He enthrones these cowards, Osmund? Were I a king, were I even a man, I would drive these smug English out of their foggy isle in three days' space! I would leave alive not one of these curs that dare yelp at me! I would—" She paused, the sudden anger veering into amusement. "See how I enrage myself when I think of what your people have made me suffer," the Queen said, and shrugged her shoulders. "In effect, I skulked back to this detestable island in disguise, accompanied by Avenel de Giars and Hubert Fitz-Herveis. To-night some half-dozen fellows—robbers, thorough knaves, like all you English,—suddenly attacked us on the common yonder and slew the men of our party. While they were cutting de Giars' throat I slipped away in the dark and tumbled through many ditches till I spied your light. There you have my story. Now get me an escort to Bristol."

It was a long while before Messire Heleigh spoke. Then, "These men," he said—"this de Giars and this Fitz-Herveis—they gave their lives for yours, as I understand it,—*pro caris amicis*. And yet you do not grieve for them."

"I shall regret de Giars," the Queen said, "for he made excellent songs. But Fitz-Herveis?—foh! the man had a face like a horse." Then again her mood changed. "Many men have died for me, my friend. At first I wept for them, but now I am dry of tears."

He shook his head. "Cato very wisely says, 'If thou hast need of help, ask it of thy friends.' But the sweet friend that I remember was a clean-eyed girl, joyous and exceedingly beautiful. Now you appear to me one of those ladies of remoter times—Faustina, or Jael, or Artemis, the King's wife of Tauris,—they that slew men, laughing. I am somewhat afraid of you, madame."

She was angry at first; then her face softened. "You English!" she said, only half mirthful. "Eh, my God! you remember me when I was happy. Now you behold me in my misery. Yet even now I am your Queen, messire, and it is not yours to pass judgment upon me."

"I do not judge you," he hastily returned. "Rather I cry with him of old, *Omnia incerta ratione*! and I cry with Salomon that he who meddles with the strife of another man is like to him that takes a hound by the ears. Yet listen, madame and Queen. I cannot afford you an escort to Bristol. This house, of which I am in temporary charge, is Longaville, my brother's manor. And Lord Brudenel, as you doubtless know, is of the barons' party and—scant cause for grief!—with Leicester at this moment. I can trust none of my brother's people, for I believe them to be of much the same opinion as those Londoners who not long ago stoned you and would have sunk your barge in Thames River. Oh, let us not blink the fact that you are not overbeloved in England. So an escort is out of the question. Yet I, madame, if you so elect, will see you safe to Bristol."

JAMES BRANCH CABELL

"You? singly?" the Queen demanded.

"My plan is this: Singing folk alone travel whither they will. We will go as jongleurs, then. I can yet manage a song to the viol, I dare affirm. And you must pass as my wife."

He said this with a very curious simplicity. The plan seemed unreasonable, and at first Dame Alianora waved it aside. Out of the question! But reflection suggested nothing better; it was impossible to remain at Longaville, and the man spoke sober truth when he declared any escort other than himself to be unprocurable. Besides, the lunar madness of the scheme was its strength; that the Queen would venture to cross half England unprotected—and Messire Heleigh on the face of him was a paste-board buckler,—was an event which Leicester would neither anticipate nor on report credit. There you were! these English had no imagination. The Queen snapped her fingers and said: "Very willingly will I be your wife, my Osmund. But how do I know that I can trust you? Leicester would give a deal for me,—any price in reason for the Sorceress of Provence. And you are not wealthy, I suspect."

"You may trust me, mon bel esper"—his eyes here were those of a beaten child,—"since my memory is better than yours." Messire Osmund Heleigh gathered his papers into a neat pile. "This room is mine. To-night I keep guard in the corridor, madame. We will start at dawn."

When he had gone, Dame Alianora laughed contentedly. "Mon bel esper! my fairest hope! The man called me that in his verses—thirty years ago! Yes, I may trust you, my poor Osmund."

So they set out at cockcrow. He had procured a viol and a long falchion for himself, and had somewhere got suitable clothes for the Queen; and in their aging but decent garb the two approached near enough to the similitude of what they desired to be esteemed. In the courtyard a knot of servants gaped, nudged one another, but openly said nothing. Messire Heleigh, as they interpreted it, was brazening out an affair of gallantry before the countryside; and they appeared to consider his casual observation that they would find a couple of dead men on the common exceedingly diverting.

When the Queen asked him the same morning: "And what will you sing, my Osmund? Shall we begin with the Sestina of Spring"? Osmund Heleigh grunted.

"I have forgotten that rubbish long ago. *Omnis amans, amens*, saith the satirist of Rome town, and with some show of reason."

Followed silence.

One sees them thus trudging the brown, naked plains under a sky of steel. In a pageant the woman, full-veined and comely, her russet gown girded up like a harvester's, might not inaptly have prefigured October; and for less comfortable November you could nowhere have found a symbol more precise than her lank companion, humorously peevish under his white thatch of hair, and so constantly fretted by the sword tapping at his ankles.

They made Hurlburt prosperously and found it vacant, for the news of Falmouth's advance had driven the villagers hillward. There was in this place a child, a naked boy of some two years, lying on a doorstep, overlooked in their gross terror. As the Queen with a sob lifted this boy the child died.

"Starved!" said Osmund Heleigh; "and within a stone's-throw of my snug home!"

The Queen laid down the tiny corpse, and, stooping, lightly caressed its sparse flaxen hair. She answered nothing, though her lips moved.

Past Vachel, scene of a recent skirmish, with many dead in the gutters, they were overtaken by Falmouth himself, and stood at the roadside to afford his troop passage. The Marquess, as he went by, flung the Queen a coin, with a jest sufficiently high-flavored. She knew the man her inveterate enemy, knew that on recognition he would have killed her as he would a wolf; she smiled at him and dropped a curtsey.

"That is very remarkable," Messire Heleigh observed. "I was hideously afraid, and am yet shaking. But you, madame, laughed."

The Queen replied: "I laughed because I know that some day I shall have Lord Falmouth's head. It will be very sweet to see it roll in the dust, my Osmund."

Messire Heleigh somewhat dryly observed that tastes differed.

At Jessop Minor a more threatening adventure befell. Seeking food at the *Cat and Hautbois* in that village, they blundered upon the same troop at dinner in the square about the inn. Falmouth and his lieutenants were somewhere inside the house. The men greeted the supposed purveyors of amusement with a shout; and one among them—a swarthy rascal with his head tied in a napkin—demanded that the jongleurs grace their meal with a song.

At first Osmund put him off with a tale of a broken viol.

But, "Haro!" the fellow blustered; "by blood and by nails! you will sing more sweetly with a broken viol than with a broken head. I would have you understand, you hedge-thief, that we gentlemen of the sword are not partial to wordy argument." Messire Heleigh fluttered inefficient hands as the men-at-arms gathered about them, scenting some genial piece of cruelty. "Oh, you rabbit!" the trooper jeered, and caught him by the throat, shaking him. In the act this rascal tore open Messire Heleigh's tunic, disclosing a thin chain about his neck and a small locket, which the fellow wrested from its fastening. "Ahoi!" he continued. "Ahoi, my comrades, what species of minstrel is this, who goes about England all hung with gold like a Cathedral Virgin! He and his sweetheart"—the actual word was grosser—"will be none the worse for an interview with the Marquess."

The situation smacked of awkwardness, for Lord Falmouth was familiar with the Queen, and to be brought specifically to his attention meant death for two detected masqueraders. Hastily Osmund Heleigh said:

"Messire, the locket contains the portrait of a lady whom in youth I loved very greatly. Save to me, it is valueless. I pray you, do not rob me of it."

But the trooper shook his head with drunken solemnity. "I do not like the looks of this. Yet I will sell it to you, as the saying is, for a song."

"It shall be the king of songs," said Osmund—"the song that Arnaut Daniel first made. I will sing for you a Sestina, messieurs—a Sestina in salutation of Spring."

The men disposed themselves about the dying grass, and presently he sang.

Sang Messire Heleigh:

> *Awaken! for the servitors of Spring*
> *Marshal his triumph! ah, make haste to see*
> *With what tempestuous pageantry they bring*
> *Mirth back to earth! hasten, for this is he*
> *That cast out Winter and the woes that cling*
> *To Winter's garments, and bade April be!*
>
> *And now that Spring is master, let us be*
> *Content, and laugh as anciently in Spring*
> *The battle-wearied Tristan laughed, when he*
> *Was come again Tintagel-ward—to bring*
> *Glad news of Arthur's victory and see*
> *Ysoude, with parted lips, that waver and cling.*

> *Anon in Brittany must Tristan cling*
> *To this or that sad memory, and be*
> *Alone, as she in Cornwall, for in Spring*
> *Love sows, and lovers reap anon—and he*
> *Is blind, and scatters baleful seed that bring*
> *Such fruitage as blind Love lacks eyes to see!*

Osmund paused here for an appreciable interval, staring at the Queen. You saw his flabby throat a-quiver, his eyes melting, saw his cheeks kindle, and youth ebb back into the lean man like water over a crumbling dam. His voice was now big and desirous.

Sang Messire Heleigh:

> *Love sows, and lovers reap; and ye will see*
> *The loved eyes lighten, feel the loved lips cling*
> *Never again when in the grave ye be*
> *Incurious of your happiness in Spring,*
> *And get no grace of Love there, whither he*
> *That bartered life for love no love may bring.*
>
> *Here Death is;—and no Heracles may bring*
> *Alcestis hence, nor here may Roland see*
> *The eyes of Aude, nor here the wakening spring*
> *Vex any man with memory, for there be*
> *No memories that cling as cerements cling,*
> *No Love that baffles Death, more strong than he.*
>
> *Us hath he noted, and for us hath he*
> *An how appointed, and that hour will bring*
> *Oblivion.—Then, laugh! Laugh, love, and see*
> *The tyrant mocked, what time our bosoms cling,*
> *What time our lips are red, what time we be*
> *Exultant in our little hour of spring!*
>
> *Thus in the spring we mock at Death, though he*
> *Will see our children perish and will bring*
> *Asunder all that cling while love may be.*

Then Osmund put the viol aside and sat quite silent. The soldiery judged, and with cordial frankness stated, that the difficulty of his

JAMES BRANCH CABELL

rhyming scheme did not atone for his lack of indecency, but when the Queen of England went among them with Messire Heleigh's hat she found them liberal. Even the fellow with the broken head admitted that a bargain was proverbially a bargain, and returned the locket with the addition of a coin. So for the present these two went safe, and quitted the *Cat and Hautbois* both fed and unmolested.

"My Osmund," Dame Alianora said, presently, "your memory is better than I had thought."

"I remembered a boy and a girl," he returned. "And I grieved that they were dead."

Afterward they plodded on toward Bowater, and the ensuing night rested in Chantrell Wood. They had the good-fortune there to encounter dry and windless weather and a sufficiency of brushwood, with which Osmund constructed an agreeable fire. In its glow these two sat, eating bread and cheese.

But talk languished at the outset. The Queen had complained of an ague, and Messire Heleigh was sedately suggesting three spiders hung about the neck as an infallible corrective for this ailment, when Dame Alianora rose to her feet.

"Eh, my God!" she said; "I am wearied of such ungracious aid! Not an inch of the way but you have been thinking of your filthy books and longing to be back at them! No; I except the moments when you were frightened into forgetfulness—first by Falmouth, then by the trooper. O Eternal Father! fraid of a single dirty soldier!"

"Indeed, I was very much afraid," said Messire Heleigh, with perfect simplicity; "*timidus perire*, madame."

"You have not even the grace to be ashamed! Yet I am shamed, messire, that Osmund Heleigh should have become the book-muddled pedant you are. For I loved him—do you understand?—I loved young Osmund Heleigh."

He also had risen in the firelight, and now its convulsive shadows marred two dogged faces. "I think it best not to recall that boy and girl who are so long dead. And, frankly, madame and Queen, the merit of the business I have in hand is questionable. It is you who have set all England by the ears, and I am guiding you toward opportunities for further mischief. I must serve you. Understand, madame, that ancient folly in Provence yonder has nothing to do with the affair. Remember that I cry *nihil ad Andromachen*! I must serve you because you are a woman and helpless; yet I cannot forget that he who spares the wolf is the sheep's murderer. It would be better for all England if you were dead. Hey, your gorgeous follies, madame! Silver peacocks set with sapphires! Cloth of fine gold—"

"Would you have me go unclothed?" Dame Alianora demanded, pettishly.

"Not so," Osmund retorted; "again I say to you with Tertullian, 'Let women paint their eyes with the tints of chastity, insert into their ears the Word of God, tie the yoke of Christ about their necks, and adorn their whole person with the silk of sanctity and the damask of devotion.' And I say to you—"

But Dame Alianora was yawning quite frankly. "You will say to me that I brought foreigners into England, that I misguided the King, that I stirred up strife between the King and his barons. Eh, my God! I am sufficiently familiar with the harangue. Yet listen, my Osmund: They sold me like a bullock to a man I had never seen. I found him a man of wax, and I remoulded him. They gave me England as a toy; I played with it. I was the Queen, the source of honor, the source of wealth—the trough, in effect, about which swine gathered. Never in all my English life, Osmund, has man or woman loved me; never in all my English life have I loved man or woman. Do you understand, my Osmund?—the Queen has many flatterers, but no friends. Not a friend in the world, my Osmund! And so the Queen makes the best of it and amuses herself."

Somewhat he seemed to understand, for he answered without asperity:

"Mon bel esper, I do not find it anywhere in Holy Writ that God requires it of us to amuse ourselves; but upon many occasions we have been commanded to live righteously. We are tempted in divers and insidious ways. And we cry with the Psalmist, 'My strength is dried up like a potsherd.' But God intends this, since, until we have here demonstrated our valor upon Satan, we are manifestly unworthy to be enregistered in His army. The great Captain must be served by proven soldiers. We may be tempted, but we may not yield, O daughter of the South! we may not yield!" he cried, with an unheralded, odd wildness.

"Again you preach," Dame Alianora said. "That is a venerable truism."

"Ho, madame," he returned, "is it on that account the less true?"

Pensively the Queen considered this. "You are a good man, my Osmund," she said at last, with a fine irrelevance, "though you are very droll. Ohime! it is a pity that I was born a princess! Had it been possible for me to be your wife, I would have been a better woman. I shall sleep

JAMES BRANCH CABELL

now and dream of that good and stupid and contented woman I might have been." So presently these two slept in Chantrell Wood.

Followed four days of journeying. As Messer Dante had not yet surveyed Malebolge, they lacked a parallel for that which they encountered; their traverse discovered England razed, charred, and depopulate—picked bones of an island, a vast and absolute ruin about which passion-wasted men skulked like rats. They went without molestation; malice and death had journeyed on their road aforetime, as heralds, and had swept it clear.

At every trace of these hideous precessors Osmund Heleigh would say, "By a day's ride I might have prevented this." Or, "By a day's ride I might have saved this woman." Or, "By two days' riding I might have fed this child."

The Queen kept Spartan silence, but daily you saw the fine woman age. In their slow advance every inch of misery was thrust before her as for inspection; meticulously she observed and appraised her handiwork.

Bastling the royal army had recently sacked. There remained of this village the skeletons of two houses, and for the rest a jumble of bricks, rafters half-burned, many calcined fragments of humanity, and ashes. At Bastling, Messire Heleigh turned to the Queen toiling behind.

"Oh, madame!" he said, in a dry whisper, "this was the home of so many men!"

"I burned it," Dame Alianora replied. "That man we passed just now I killed. Those other men and women—my folly killed them all. And little children, my Osmund! The hair like corn-floss, blood-dabbled!"

"Oh, madame!" he wailed, in the extremity of his pity.

For she stood with eyes shut, all gray. The Queen demanded: "Why have they not slain me? Was there no man in England to strangle the proud wanton? Are you all cowards here?"

"Not cowards!" he cried. "Your men and Leicester's ride about the world, and draw sword and slay and die for the right as they see it. And you for the right as ye see it. But I, madame! I! I, who sat snug at home spilling ink and trimming rose-bushes! God's world, madame, and I in it afraid to speak a word for Him! God's world, and a curmudgeon in it grudging God the life He gave!" The man flung out his soft hands and snarled: "We are tempted in divers and insidious ways. But I, who rebuked you! behold, now, with how gross a snare was I entrapped!"

"I do not understand, my Osmund."

"I was afraid, madame," he returned, dully. "Everywhere men fight and I am afraid to die."

So they stood silent in the ruins of Bastling.

"Of a piece with our lives," Dame Alianora said at last. "All ruin, my Osmund."

But Messire Heleigh threw back his head and laughed, new color in his face. "Presently men will build here, my Queen. Presently, as in legend the Arabian bird, arises from these ashes a lordlier and more spacious town."

Then they went forward. The next day Fate loosed upon them Gui Camoys, lord of Bozon, Foliot, and Thwenge, who, riding alone through Poges Copse, found there a man and a woman over their limited supper. The woman had thrown back her hood, and Camoys drew rein to stare at her. Lispingly he spoke the true court dialect.

"Ma belle," said this Camoys, in friendly condescension, "n'estez vous pas jongleurs?"

Dame Alianora smiled up at him. "Ouais, messire; mon mary faict les chancons—" Here she paused, with dilatory caution, for Camoys had leaped from his horse, giving a great laugh.

"A prize! ho, an imperial prize!" Camoys shouted. "A peasant woman with the Queen's face, who speaks French! And who, madame, is this? Have you by any chance brought pious Lewis from oversea? Have I bagged a brace of monarchs?"

Here was imminent danger, for Camoys had known the Queen some fifteen years. Messire Heleigh rose to his feet, his five days' beard glinting like hoar-frost as his mouth twitched.

"I am Osmund Heleigh, messire, younger brother to the Earl of Brudenel."

"I have heard of you, I believe—the fellow who spoils parchment. This is odd company, however, Messire Osmund, for Brudenel's brother."

"A gentleman must serve his Queen, messire. As Cicero very justly observes—"

"I am inclined to think that his political opinions are scarcely to our immediate purpose. This is a high matter, Messire Heleigh. To let the sorceress pass is, of course, out of the question; upon the other hand, I observe that you lack weapons of defence. Yet if you will have the kindness to assist me in unarming, your courtesy will place our commerce on more equal footing."

Osmund had gone very white. "I am no swordsman, messire—"

"Now, this is not handsome of you," Camoys began. "I warn you that people will speak harshly of us if we lose this opportunity of gaining honor. And besides, the woman will be burned. Plainly, you owe it to all three of us to fight."

"—but I refer my cause to God. I am quite at your service."

"No, my Osmund!" Dame Alianora then cried. "It means your death."

He spread out his hands. "That is God's affair, madame."

"Are you not afraid?" she breathed.

"Of course I am afraid," said Messire Heleigh, irritably.

After that he unarmed Camoys, and presently they faced each other in their tunics. So for the first time in the journey Osmund's long falchion saw daylight. He had thrown away his dagger, as Camoys had none.

The combat was sufficiently curious. Camoys raised his left hand. "So help me God and His saints, I have upon me neither bone, stone, nor witchcraft wherethrough the power and the word of God might be diminished or the devil's power increased."

Osmund made similar oath. "Judge Thou this woman's cause!" he cried, likewise.

Then Gui Camoys shouted, as a herald might have done, "Laissez les aller, laissez les aller, laissez les aller, les bons combatants!" and warily each moved toward the other.

On a sudden Osmund attacked, desperately apprehensive of his own cowardice. Camoys lightly eluded him and slashed his undefended thigh, drawing much blood. Osmund gasped. He flung away his sword, and in the instant catching Camoys under the arms, threw him to the ground. Messire Heleigh fell with his opponent, who in stumbling had lost his sword, and thus the two struggled unarmed, Osmund atop. But Camoys was the younger man, and Osmund's strength was ebbing rapidly by reason of his wound. Now Camoys' tethered horse, rearing with nervousness, tumbled his master's flat-topped helmet into the road. Osmund caught it up and with it battered Camoys in the face, dealing severe blows.

"God!" Camoys cried, his face all blood.

"Do you acknowledge my quarrel just?" said Osmund, between horrid sobs.

"What choice have I?" said Gui Camoys, very sensibly.

So Osmund rose, blind with tears and shivering. The Queen bound up their wounds as best she might, but Camoys was much dissatisfied.

"For reasons of His own, madame," he observed, "and doubtless for sufficient ones, God has singularly favored your cause. I am neither a fool nor a pagan to question His decision, and you two may go your way unhampered. But I have had my head broken with my own helmet, and this I consider to be a proceeding very little conducive toward enhancing my reputation. Of your courtesy, messire, I must entreat another meeting."

Osmund shrank as from a blow. Then, with a short laugh, he conceded that this was Camoys' right, and they fixed upon the following Saturday, with Poges Copse as the rendezvous.

"I would suggest that the combat be a outrance," Gui Camoys said, "in consideration of the fact it was my own helmet. You must undoubtedly be aware, Messire Osmund, that such an affront is practically without any parallel."

This, too, was agreed upon, and they bade one another farewell.

Then, after asking if they needed money, which was courteously declined, Gui Camoys rode away, and sang as he went. Osmund Heleigh remained motionless. He raised quivering hands to the sky.

"Thou hast judged!" he cried. "Thou hast judged, O puissant Emperor of Heaven! Now pardon! Pardon us twain! Pardon for unjust stewards of Thy gifts! Thou hast loaned this woman dominion over England, all instruments to aid Thy cause, and this trust she has abused. Thou hast loaned me life and manhood, agility and wit and strength, all instruments to aid Thy cause. Talents in a napkin, O God! Repentant we cry to Thee. Pardon for unjust stewards! Pardon for the ungirt loin, for the service shirked, for all good deeds undone! Pardon and grace, O King of kings!"

Thus he prayed, while Gui Camoys sang, riding deeper into the tattered, yellowing forest. By an odd chance Camoys had lighted on that song made by Thibaut of Champagne, beginning *Signor, saciez, ki or ne s'en ira*, and this he sang with a lilt gayer than the matter of it countenanced. Faintly there now came to them the sound of his singing, and they found it, in the circumstances, ominously adapt.

Sang Camoys:

> *Et vos, par qui je n'oi onques aie,*
> *Descendez tuit en infer le par font.*

　　　　　　　　　　　　　JAMES BRANCH CABELL

Dame Alianora shivered. "No, no!" she cried. "Is He less pitiful than we?"

They slept that night in Ousley Meadow, and the next afternoon came safely to Bristol. You may learn elsewhere with what rejoicing the royal army welcomed the Queen's arrival, how courage quickened at sight of the generous virago. In the ebullition Messire Heleigh was submerged, and Dame Alianora saw nothing more of him that day. Friday there were counsels, requisitions, orders signed, a memorial despatched to Pope Urban, chief of all a letter (this in the Queen's hand throughout) privily conveyed to the Lady Maude de Mortemer—much sowing of a seed, in fine, that eventually flowered victory. There was, however, no sign of Osmund Heleigh, though by Dame Alianora's order he was sought.

On Saturday at seven in the morning he came to her lodging in complete armor. From the open helmet his wrinkled face, showing like a wizened nut in a shell, smiled upon her questionings.

"I go to fight Gui Camoys, madame and Queen."

Dame Alianora wrung her hands. "You go to your death."

He answered: "That is very likely. Therefore I am come to bid you farewell."

The Queen stared at him for a while; on a sudden she broke into a curious fit of deep but tearless sobbing.

"Mon bel esper," said Osmund Heleigh, very gently, "what is there in all this worthy of your sorrow? The man will kill me; granted, for he is my junior by some fifteen years, and in addition a skilled swordsman. I fail to see that this is lamentable. Back to Longaville I cannot go after recent happenings; there a rope's end awaits me. Here I must in any event shortly take to the sword, since a beleaguered army has very little need of ink-pots; and shortly I must be slain in some skirmish, dug under the ribs perhaps by a greasy fellow I have never seen. I prefer a clean death at a gentleman's hands."

"It is I who bring about your death!" she wailed. "You gave me gallant service, and I have requited you with death!"

"Indeed the debt is on the other side. The trivial services I rendered you were such as any gentleman must render a woman in distress. Naught else have I afforded you, madame, save very anciently a Sestina. Ho, a Sestina! And in return you have given me a Sestina of fairer make—a Sestina of days, six days of life." His eyes were fervent now.

She kissed him on either cheek. "Farewell, my champion!"

"Ay, your champion. In the twilight of life old Osmund Heleigh rides forth to defend the quarrel of Alianora of Provence. Reign wisely, my Queen, that hereafter men may not say I was slain in an evil cause. Do not shame my maiden venture."

"I will not shame you," the Queen proudly said; and then, with a change of voice: "O my Osmund! My Osmund!"

He caught her by each wrist. "Hush!" he bade her, roughly; and stood crushing both her hands to his lips, with fierce staring. "Wife of my King! wife of my King!" he babbled; and then flung her from him, crying, with a great lift of speech: "I have not failed you! Praise God, I have not failed you!"

From her window she saw him ride away, a rich flush of glitter and color. In new armor with a smart emblazoned surcoat the lean pedant sat conspicuously erect, though by this the fear of death had gripped him to the marrow; and as he went he sang defiantly, taunting the weakness of his flesh.

Sang Osmund Heleigh:

> *Love sows, and lovers reap; and ye will see*
> *The loved eyes lighten, feel the loved lips cling*
> *Never again when in the grave ye be*
> *Incurious of your happiness in spring,*
> *And get no grace of Love there, whither he*
> *That bartered life for love no love may bring.*

So he rode away and thus out of our history. But in the evening Gui Camoys came into Bristol under a flag of truce, and behind him heaved a litter wherein lay Osmund Heleigh's body.

"For the man was a brave one," Camoys said to the Queen, "and in the matter of the reparation he owed me acted very handsomely. It is fitting that he should have honorable interment."

"That he shall not lack," the Queen said, and gently unclasped from Osmund's neck the thin gold chain, now locketless. "There was a portrait here," she said; "the portrait of a woman whom he loved in his youth, Messire Camoys. And all his life it lay above his heart."

Camoys answered stiffly: "I imagine this same locket to have been the object which Messire Heleigh flung into the river, shortly before we began our combat. I do not rob the dead, madame."

"The act was very like him," the Queen said. "Messire Camoys, I think that this day is a festival in heaven."

Afterward she set to work on requisitions in the King's name. But Osmund Heleigh she had interred at Ambresbury, commanding it to be written on his tomb that he died in the Queen's cause.

How the same cause prospered (Nicolas concludes), how presently Dame Alianora reigned again in England and with what wisdom, and how in the end this great Queen died a nun at Ambresbury and all England wept therefor—this you may learn elsewhere. I have chosen to record six days of a long and eventful life; and (as Messire Heleigh might have done) I say modestly with him of old, *Majores majora sonent*. Nevertheless, I assert that many a forest was once a pocketful of acorns.

THE END OF THE FIRST NOVEL

II

The Story of the Tenson

In the year of grace 1265 (Nicolas begins), about the festival of Saint Peter *ad Vincula*, the Prince de Gatinais came to Burgos. Before this he had lodged for three months in the district of Ponthieu; and the object of his southern journey was to assure the tenth Alphonso, then ruling in Castile, that the latter's sister Ellinor, now resident at Entrechat, was beyond any reasonable doubt the transcendent lady whose existence old romancers had anticipated, however cloudily, when they fabled in remote time concerning Queen Heleine of Sparta.

There was a postscript to his news, and a pregnant one. The world knew that the King of Leon and Castile desired to be King of Germany as well, and that at present a single vote in the Diet would decide between his claims and those of his competitor, Earl Richard of Cornwall. De Gatinais chaffered fairly; he had a vote, Alphonso had a sister. So that, in effect—ohe, in effect, he made no question that his Majesty understood!

The Astronomer twitched his beard and demanded if the fact that Ellinor had been a married woman these ten years past was not an obstacle to the plan which his fair cousin had proposed?

Here the Prince was accoutred cap-a-pie, and in consequence hauled out a paper. Dating from Viterbo, Clement, Bishop of Rome, servant to the servants of God, desirous of all health and apostolical blessing for his well-beloved son in Christ, stated that a compact between a boy of fifteen and a girl of ten was an affair of no particular moment; and that in consideration of the covenanters never having clapped eyes upon each other since the wedding-day—even had not the precontract of marriage between the groom's father and the bride's mother rendered a consummation of the childish oath an obvious and a most heinous enormity—why, that, in a sentence, and for all his coy verbosity, the new pontiff was perfectly amenable to reason.

So in a month it was settled. Alphonso would give his sister to de Gatinais, and in exchange get the latter's vote; and Gui Foulques of Sabionetta—now Clement, fourth Pope to assume that name—would annul the previous marriage, they planned, and in exchange get an

JAMES BRANCH CABELL

armament to serve him against Manfred, the late and troublesome tyrant of Sicily and Apulia. The scheme promised to each one of them that which he in particular desired, and messengers were presently sent into Ponthieu.

It is now time we put aside these Castilian matters and speak of other things. In England, Prince Edward had fought, and won, a shrewd battle at Evesham; the barons' power was demolished, there would be no more internecine war; and spurred by the unaccustomed idleness, he began to think of the foreign girl he had not seen since the day he wedded her. She would be a woman by this, and it was befitting that he claim his wife. He rode with Hawise d'Ebernoe to Ambresbury, and at the gate of the nunnery they parted, with what agonies are immaterial to this history's progression; the tale merely tells that latterly the Prince went into Lower Picardy alone, riding at adventure as he loved to do, and thus came to Entrechat, where his wife resided with her mother, the Countess Johane.

In a wood near the castle he approached a company of Spaniards, four in number, their horses tethered while these men (Oviedans, as they told him) drank about a great stone which served them for a table. Being thirsty, he asked and was readily accorded hospitality, so that within the instant these five fell into an amicable discourse. One fellow asked his name and business in those parts, and the Prince gave each without hesitancy as he reached for the bottle, and afterward dropped it just in time to catch, cannily, with his naked left hand, the knife-blade with which the rascal had dug at the unguarded ribs. The Prince was astounded, but he was never a subtle man: here were four knaves who, for reasons unexplained—but to them of undoubted cogency—desired the death of Sire Edward, the King of England's son: and manifestly there was here an actionable difference of opinion; so he had his sword out and presently killed the four of them.

Anon there came to him an apple-cheeked boy, habited as a page, who, riding jauntily through the forest, lighted upon the Prince, now in bottomless vexation. The lad drew rein, and his lips outlined a whistle. At his feet were several dead men in a very untidy condition. And seated among them, as throned upon the boulder, was a gigantic and florid person, so tall that the heads of few people reached to his shoulder; a person of handsome exterior, blond, and chested like a stallion, whose left eyebrow drooped so oddly that even in anger the stupendous man appeared to assure you, quite confidentially, that the dilapidation he threatened was an excellent jest.

"Fair friend," said the page. "God give you joy! and why have you converted this forest into a shambles?"

The Prince told him of the half-hour's action as has been narrated. "I have perhaps been rather hasty," he considered by way of peroration, "and it vexes me that I did not spare, say, one of these lank Spaniards, if only long enough to ascertain why, in the name of Termagaunt, they should have desired my destruction."

But midway in his talc the boy had dismounted with a gasp, and he was now inspecting the features of one carcass. "Felons, my Prince! You have slain some eight yards of felony which might have cheated the gallows had they got the Princess Ellinor safe to Burgos. Only two days ago this chalk-eyed fellow conveyed to her a letter."

Prince Edward said, "You appear, lad, to be somewhat over heels in the confidence of my wife."

Now the boy arose and defiantly flung back his head in shrill laughter. "Your wife! Oh, God ha' mercy! Your wife, and for ten years left to her own devices! Why, look you, to-day you and your wife would not know each other were you twain brought face to face."

Prince Edward said, "That is very near the truth." But, indeed, it was the absolute truth, and as concerned himself already attested.

"Sire Edward," the boy then said, "your wife has wearied of this long waiting till you chose to whistle for her. Last summer the young Prince de Gatinais came a-wooing—and he is a handsome man." The page made known all which de Gatinais and King Alphonso planned, the words jostling as they came in torrents, but so that one might understand. "I am her page, my lord. I was to follow her. These fellows were to be my escort, were to ward off possible pursuit. Cry haro, beau sire! Cry haro, and lustily, for your wife in company with six other knaves is at large between here and Burgos—that unreasonable wife who grew dissatisfied after a mere ten years of neglect."

"I have been remiss," the Prince said, and one huge hand strained at his chin; "yes, perhaps I have been remiss. Yet it had appeared to me— But as it is, I bid you mount, my lad!" he cried, in a new voice.

The boy demanded, "And to what end?"

"Oy Dieus, messire! have I not slain your escort? Why, in common reason, equity demands that I afford you my protection so far as Burgos, messire, just as equity demands I on arrival slay de Gatinais and fetch back my wife to England."

The page wrung exquisite hands with a gesture which was but partially tinged with anguish and presently began to laugh. Afterward these two rode southerly, in the direction of Castile.

For it appeared to the intriguing little woman a diverting jest that in this fashion her husband should be the promoter of her evasion. It appeared to her more diverting when in two days' space she had become genuinely fond of him. She found him rather slow of comprehension, and was namelessly humiliated by the discovery that not an eyelash of the man was irritated by his wife's decampment; he considered, to all appearances, that some property of his had been stolen, and he intended, quite without passion, to repossess himself of it, after, of course, punishing the thief.

This troubled the Princess somewhat; and often, riding by his more stolid side, the girl's heart raged at memory of the decade so newly overpast which had kept her always dependent on the charity of this or that ungracious patron—on any one who would take charge of her while the truant husband fought out his endless squabbles in England. Slights enough she had borne during the period, and squalor, and hunger even. But now at last she rode toward the dear southland; and presently she would be rid of this big man, when he had served her purpose; and afterward she meant to wheedle Alphonso, just as she had always done, and later still she and Etienne would be very happy; and, in fine, to-morrow was to be a new day.

So these two rode ever southward, and always Prince Edward found this new page of his—this Miguel de Rueda—a jolly lad, who whistled and sang inapposite snatches of balladry, without any formal ending or beginning, descanting always with the delicate irrelevancy of a bird-trill. Sang Miguel de Rueda:

> *Lord Love, that leads me day by day*
> *Through many a screened and scented way,*
> *Finds to assuage my thirst*
> *No love that may the old love slay,*
> *None sweeter than the first.*

> *Ah, heart of mine, that beats so fast*
> *As this or that fair maid trips past,*
> *Once and with lesser stir*
> *We spied the heart's-desire, at last,*
> *And turned, and followed her.*

For Love had come that in the spring
When all things woke to blossoming
Was as a child that came
Laughing, and filled with wondering,
Nor knowing his own name—

"And still I would prefer to think," the big man interrupted, heavily, "that Sicily is not the only allure. I would prefer to think my wife so beautiful—And yet, as I remember her, she was nothing extraordinary."

The page a little tartly said that people might forget a deal within a decade.

For the Prince had quickly fathomed the meaning of the scheme hatched in Castile. "When Manfred is driven out of Sicily they will give the throne to de Gatinais. He intends to get both a kingdom and a handsome wife by this neat affair. And in reason England must support my uncle against El Sabio. Why, my lad, I ride southward to prevent a war that would convulse half Europe."

"You ride southward in the attempt to rob a miserable woman of her sole chance of happiness," Miguel de Rueda estimated.

"That is undeniable, if she loves this thrifty Prince, as indeed I do not question my wife does. Yet is our happiness here a trivial matter, whereas war is a great disaster. You have not seen—as I have done, my little Miguel—a man viewing his death-wound with a face of stupid wonder?—a man about to die in his lord's quarrel and understanding never a word of it? Or a woman, say—a woman's twisted and naked body, the breasts yet horribly heaving, in the red ashes of some village? or the already dripping hoofs which will presently crush this body? Well, it is to prevent a many such spectacles hereabout that I ride southward."

Miguel de Rueda shuddered. But, "She has her right to happiness," the page stubbornly said.

"Not so," the Prince retorted; "since it hath pleased the Emperor of Heaven to appoint us twain to lofty stations, to intrust to us the five talents of the parable; whence is our debt to Him, being fivefold, so much the greater than that of common persons. And therefore the more is it our sole right, being fivefold, to serve God without faltering, and therefore is our happiness, or our unhappiness, the more an inconsiderable matter. For as I have read in the Annals of the Romans—" He launched upon the story of King Pompey and his daughter, whom a certain duke regarded with impure and improper emotions. "My little Miguel, that ancient king is our Heavenly Father, that only daughter is the rational soul of us, which is here delivered for protection to five soldiers—that is, to the five senses—to preserve it from the devil, the world, and the flesh. But, alas! the too-credulous soul, desirous of gazing upon the gaudy vapors of this world—"

"You whine like a canting friar," the page complained; "and I can assure you that the Lady Ellinor was prompted rather than hindered by her God-given faculties of sight and hearing and so on when she fell in love with de Gatinais. Of you two, he is, beyond any question, the handsomer and the more intelligent man, and it was God who bestowed on her sufficient wit to perceive the fact. And what am I to deduce from this?"

The Prince reflected. At last he said: "I have also read in these same Gestes how Seneca mentions that in poisoned bodies, on account of the malignancy and the coldness of the poison, no worm will engender; but if the body be smitten by lightning, in a few days the carcass will abound with vermin. My little Miguel, both men and women are at birth empoisoned by sin, and then they produce no worm—that is, no virtue; but struck with lightning—that is, by the grace of God—they are astonishingly fruitful in good works."

The page began to laugh. "You are hopelessly absurd, my Prince, though you will never know it—and I hate you a little—and I envy you a great deal."

"Nay," Prince Edward said, in misapprehension, for the man was never quick-witted—"nay, it is not for my own happiness that I ride southward."

The page then said. "What is her name?"

And Prince Edward answered, very fondly, "Hawise."

"Her, too, I hate," said Miguel de Rueda; "and I think that the holy angels alone know how profoundly I envy her."

In the afternoon of the same day they neared Ruffec, and at the ford found three brigands ready, two of whom the Prince slew, and the other fled.

Next night they supped at Manneville, and sat afterward in the little square, tree-chequered, that lay before their inn. Miguel had procured a lute from the innkeeper, and strummed idly as these two debated together of great matters; about them was an immeasurable twilight, moonless, but tempered by many stars, and everywhere an agreeable conference of leaves.

"Listen, my Prince," the boy said more lately: "here is one view of the affair." And he began to chant, without rhyming, without raising his voice above the pitch of talk, what time the lute monotonously sobbed beneath his fingers.

Sang Miguel:

A little while and Irus and Menephtah are at sorry unison, and Guenevere is but a skull. Multitudinously we tread toward oblivion, as ants hasten toward sugar, and presently Time cometh with his broom. Multitudinously we tread a dusty road toward oblivion; but yonder the sun shines upon a grass-plot, converting it into an emerald; and I am aweary of the trodden path.

Vine-crowned is she that guards the grasses yonder, and her breasts are naked. "Vanity of Vanities!" saith the beloved. But she whom I love seems very far away to-night, though I might be with her if I would. And she may not aid me now, for not even love is all-powerful. She is fairest of created women, and very wise, but she may never understand that at any time one grows aweary of the trodden path.

Yet though she cannot understand, this woman who has known me to the marrow, I must obey her laudable behests and serve her blindly. At sight of her my love closes over my heart like a flood, so that I am speechless and glory in my impotence, as one who stands at last before the kindly face of God. For her sake I have striven, with a good endeavor, to my tiny uttermost. Pardie, I am not Priam at the head of his army! A little while and I will repent; to-night I cannot but remember that there are women whose lips are of a livelier tint, that life is short at best, that wine is a goodly thing, and that I am aweary of the trodden path.

She is very far from me to-night. Yonder in the Horselberg they exult and make sweet songs, songs which are sweeter, immeasurably sweeter, than this song of mine, but in the trodden path I falter, for I am tired, tired in every fibre o' me, and I am aweary of the trodden path.

Followed a silence. "Ignorance spoke there," the Prince said. "It is the song of a woman, or else of a boy who is very young. Give me the lute, my little Miguel." And presently he, too, sang.

Sang the Prince:

I was in a path, and I trod toward the citadel of the land's Seigneur, and on either side were pleasant and forbidden meadows, having various names. And one trod with me who babbled of the brooding mountains and of the low-lying and adjacent clouds; of the west wind and of the budding fruit-trees; and he debated the significance of these things, and he went astray to gather violets, while I walked in the trodden path.

He babbled of genial wine and of the alert lips of women, of swinging censers and of pale-mouthed priests, and his heart was troubled by a world profuse in beauty. And he leaped a stile to share his allotted provision with a dying dog, and afterward, being hungry, a wall to pilfer apples, what while I walked in the trodden path.

He babbled of Autumn's bankruptcy and of the age-long lying promises of Spring; and of his own desire to be at rest; and of running waters and of decaying leaves. He babbled of the far-off stars; and he debated whether they were the eyes of God or gases which burned, and he demonstrated, very clearly, that neither existed; and at times he stumbled as he stared about him and munched his apples, so that he was all bemired, but I walked in the trodden path.

And the path led to the gateway of a citadel, and through the gateway. "Let us not enter," he said, "for the citadel is vacant, and, moreover, I am in profound terror, and, besides, as yet I have not eaten all my apples." And he wept aloud, but I was not afraid, for I had walked in the trodden path.

Again there was a silence. "You paint a dreary world, my Prince."

"Nay, my little Miguel, I do but paint the world as the Eternal Father made it. The laws of the place are written large, so that all may read them; and we know that every path, whether it be my trodden one or some byway through your gayer meadows, yet leads in the end to God. We have our choice—or to come to Him as a laborer comes at evening for the day's wages fairly earned, or to come as some roisterer haled before the magistrate."

"I consider you to be in the right," the boy said, after a lengthy interval, "although I decline—and emphatically—to believe you."

The Prince laughed. "There spoke Youth," he said, and he sighed as though he were a patriarch; "but we have sung, we two, the Eternal Tenson of God's will and of man's desires. And I claim the prize, my little Miguel."

Suddenly the page kissed one huge hand. "You have conquered, my very dull and very glorious Prince. Concerning that Hawise—" but

Miguel de Rueda choked. "Oh, I understand! in part I understand!" the page wailed, and now it was Prince Edward who comforted Miguel de Rueda.

For the Prince laid one hand upon his page's hair, and smiled in the darkness to note how soft it was, since the man was less a fool than at first view you might have taken him to be, and said:

"One must play the game, my lad. We are no little people, she and I, the children of many kings, of God's regents here on earth; and it was never reasonable, my Miguel, that gentlefolk should cog at dice."

The same night Miguel de Rueda sobbed through the prayer which Saint Theophilus made long ago to the Mother of God:

> *Dame, je n'ose,*
> *Flors d'aiglentier et lis et rose,*
> *En qui li filz Diex se repose,*

and so on. Or, in other wording: "Hearken, O gracious Lady! thou that art more fair than any flower of the eglantine, more comely than the blossoming of the rose or of the lily! thou to whom was confided the very Son of God! Hearken, for I am afraid! afford counsel to me that am ensnared by Satan and know not what to do! Never will I make an end of praying. O Virgin debonnaire! O honored Lady! Thou that wast once a woman—!"

You would have said the boy was dying; and in sober verity a deal of Miguel de Rueda died upon this night of clearer vision.

Yet he sang the next day as these two rode southward, although half as in defiance.

Sang Miguel:

> *And still, whate'er the years may send—*
> *Though Time be proven a fickle friend,*
> *And Love be shown a liar—*
> *I must adore until the end*
> *That primal heart's desire.*
>
> *I may not 'hear men speak of her*
> *Unmoved, and vagrant pulses stir*
> *Whene'er she passes by,*
> *And I again her worshipper*
> *Must serve her till I die.*

Not she that is doth pass, but she
That Time hath riven away from me
And in the darkness set—
The maid that I may never see,
Or gain, or e'er forget.

It was on the following day, near Bazas, these two encountered Adam de Gourdon, a Provencal knight, with whom the Prince fought for a long while, without either contestant giving way; and in consequence a rendezvous was fixed for the November of that year, and afterward the Prince and de Gourdon parted, highly pleased with each other.

Thus the Prince and his attendant came, in late September, to Mauleon, on the Castilian frontier, and dined there at the *Fir Cone*. Three or four lackeys were about—some exalted person's retinue? Prince Edward hazarded to the swart little landlord as the Prince and Miguel lingered over the remnants of their meal.

Yes, the fellow informed them: the Prince de Gatinais had lodged there for a whole week, watching the north road, as circumspect of all passage as a cat over a mouse-hole. Eh, monseigneur expected some one, doubtless—a lady, it might be—the gentlefolk had their escapades like every one else. The innkeeper babbled vaguely, for on a sudden he was very much afraid of his gigantic patron.

"You will show me to his room," Prince Edward said, with a politeness that was ingratiating.

The host shuddered and obeyed.

Miguel de Rueda, left alone, sat quite silent, his fingertips drumming upon the table. He rose suddenly and flung back his shoulders, all resolution to the tiny heels. On the stairway he passed the black little landlord.

"I think," the little landlord considered, "that Saint Michael must have been of similar appearance when he went to meet the Evil One. Ho, messire, will there be bloodshed?"

But Miguel de Rueda had passed to the room above. The door was ajar. He paused there.

De Gatinais had risen from his dinner and stood facing the door. He, too, was a blond man and the comeliest of his day. And at sight of him awoke in the woman's heart all of the old tenderness; handsome and brave and witty she knew him to be, past reason, as indeed the whole world knew him to be distinguished by every namable grace; and the innate weakness of de Gatinais, which she alone suspected, made him now seem doubly dear. Fiercely she wanted to shield him, less from carnal injury than from that self-degradation she cloudily apprehended to be at hand; the test was come, and Etienne would fail. Thus much she knew with a sick, illimitable surety, and she loved de Gatinais with a passion which dwarfed comprehension.

"O Madame the Virgin!" prayed Miguel de Rueda, "thou that wast once a woman, even as I am now a woman! grant that the man may slay him quickly! grant that he may slay Etienne very quickly, honored Lady, so that my Etienne may die unshamed!"

"I must question, messire," de Gatinais was saying, "whether you have been well inspired. Yes, quite frankly, I do await the arrival of her who is your nominal wife; and your intervention at this late stage, I take it, can have no outcome save to render you absurd. Nay, rather be advised by me, messire—"

Prince Edward said, "I am not here to talk."

"For, messire, I grant you that in ordinary disputation the cutting of one gentleman's throat by another gentleman is well enough, since the argument is unanswerable. Yet in this case we have each of us too much to live for; you to govern your reconquered England, and I—you perceive that I am candid—to achieve in turn the kingship of another realm. And to secure this, possession of the Lady Ellinor is to me essential; to you she is nothing."

"She is a woman whom I have deeply wronged," Prince Edward said, "and to whom, God willing, I mean to make atonement. Ten years ago they wedded us, willy-nilly, to avert the impending war 'twixt Spain and England; to-day El Sabio intends to purchase all Germany, with her body as the price, you to get Sicily as her husband. Mort de Dieu! is a woman thus to be bought and sold like hog's-flesh! We have other and cleaner customs, we of England."

"Eh, and who purchased the woman first?" de Gatinais spat at him, and viciously, for the Frenchman now saw his air-castle shaken to the corner-stone.

"They wedded me to the child in order a great war might be averted. I acquiesced, since it appeared preferable that two people suffer inconvenience rather than many thousands be slain. And still this is my view of the matter. Yet afterward I failed her. Love had no clause in our agreement; but I owed her more protection than I have afforded. England has long been no place for women. I thought she would comprehend that much. But I know very little of women. Battle and death are more

JAMES BRANCH CABELL

wholesome companions, I now perceive, than such folk as you and Alphonso. Woman is the weaker vessel—the negligence was mine—I may not blame her." The big and simple man was in an agony of repentance.

On a sudden he strode forward, his sword now shifted to his left hand and his right hand outstretched. "One and all, we are but weaklings in the net of circumstance. Shall one herring, then, blame his fellow if his fellow jostle him? We walk as in a mist of error, and Belial is fertile in allurements; yet always it is granted us to behold that sin is sin. I have perhaps sinned through anger, Messire de Gatinais, more deeply than you have planned to sin through luxury and through ambition. Let us then cry quits, Messire de Gatinais, and afterward part in peace, and in common repentance, if you so elect."

"And yield you Ellinor?" de Gatinais said. "Nay, messire, I reply to you with Arnaud de Marveil, that marvellous singer of eld, 'They may bear her from my presence, but they can never untie the knot which unites my heart to her; for that heart, so tender and so constant, God alone divides with my lady, and the portion which God possesses He holds but as a part of her domain, and as her vassal.'"

"This is blasphemy," Prince Edward now retorted, "and for such observations alone you merit death. Will you always talk and talk and talk? I perceive that the devil is far more subtle than you, messire, and leads you like a pig with a ring in his nose toward gross iniquity. Messire, I tell you that for your soul's health I doubly mean to kill you now. So let us make an end of this."

De Gatinais turned and took up his sword. "Since you will have it," he rather regretfully said; "yet I reiterate that you play an absurd part. Your wife has deserted you, has fled in abhorrence of you. For three weeks she has been tramping God knows whither or in what company—"

He was here interrupted. "What the Lady Ellinor has done," Prince Edward crisply said, "was at my request. We were wedded at Burgos; it was most natural that we should desire our reunion to take place at Burgos; and she came to Burgos with an escort which I provided."

De Gatinais sneered. "So that is the tale you will deliver to the world?"

"When I have slain you," the Prince said, "yes. Yes, since she is a woman, and woman is the weaker vessel."

"The reservation is wise. For once I am dead, Messire Edward, there will be none to know that you risk all for a drained goblet, for an orange already squeezed—quite dry, messire."

"Face of God!" the Prince said.

But de Gatinais flung back both arms in a great gesture, so that he knocked a flask of claret from the table at his rear. "I am candid, my Prince. I would not see any brave gentleman slain in a cause so foolish. And in consequence I kiss and tell. In effect, I was eloquent, I was magnificent—so that in the end her reserve was shattered like the wooden flask yonder at our feet. Is it worth while, think you, that our blood flow like this flagon's contents?"

"Liar!" Prince Edward said, very softly. "O hideous liar! Already your eyes shift!" He drew near and struck the Frenchman. "Talk and talk and talk! and lying talk! I am ashamed while I share the world with a thing so base as you."

De Gatinais hurled upon him, cursing, sobbing in an abandoned fury. In an instant the place resounded like a smithy, for there were no better swordsmen living than these two. The eavesdropper could see nothing clearly. Round and round they veered in a whirl of turmoil. Presently Prince Edward trod upon the broken flask, smashing it. His foot slipped in the spilth of wine, and the huge body went down like an oak, the head of it striking one leg of the table.

"A candle!" de Gatinais cried, and he panted now—"a hundred candles to the Virgin of Beaujolais!" He shortened his sword to stab the Prince of England.

And now the eavesdropper understood. She flung open the door and fell upon Prince Edward, embracing him. The sword dug deep into her shoulder, so that she shrieked once with the cold pain of this wound. Then she rose, all ashen.

"Liar!" she said. "Oh, I am shamed while I share the world with a thing so base as you!"

In silence de Gatinais regarded her. There was a long interval before he said, "Ellinor!" and then again, "Ellinor!" like a man bewildered.

"*I was eloquent, I was magnificent,*" she said, "*so that in the end her reserve was shattered!* Certainly, messire, it is not your death which I desire, since a man dies so very, very quickly. I desire for you—I know not what I desire for you!" the girl wailed.

"You desire that I should endure this present moment," de Gatinais said; "for as God reigns, I love you, and now am I shamed past death."

She said: "And I, too, loved you. It is strange to think of that."

"I was afraid. Never in my life have I been afraid before. But I was afraid of this terrible and fair and righteous man. I saw all hope of you vanish, all hope of Sicily—in effect, I lied as a cornered beast spits out his venom," de Gatinais said.

"I know," she answered. "Give me water, Etienne." She washed and bound the Prince's head with a vinegar-soaked napkin. Ellinor sat upon the floor, the big man's head upon her knee. "He will not die of this, for he is of strong person. Look you, Messire de Gatinais, you and I are not. We are so fashioned that we can enjoy only the pleasant things of life. But this man can enjoy—enjoy, mark you—the commission of any act, however distasteful, if he think it to be his duty. There is the difference. I cannot fathom him. But it is now necessary that I become all which he loves—since he loves it—and that I be in thought and deed all which he desires. For I have heard the Tenson through."

"You love him!" said de Gatinais.

She glanced upward with a pitiable smile. "Nay, it is you that I love, my Etienne. You cannot understand—can you?—how at this very moment every fibre of me—heart, soul, and body—may be longing just to comfort you and to give you all which you desire, my Etienne, and to make you happy, my handsome Etienne, at however dear a cost. No; you will never understand that. And since you may not understand, I merely bid you go and leave me with my husband."

And then there fell between these two an infinite silence.

"Listen," de Gatinais said; "grant me some little credit for what I do. You are alone; the man is powerless. My fellows are within call. A word secures the Prince's death; a word gets me you and Sicily. And I do not speak that word, for you are my lady as well as his."

But there was no mercy in the girl, no more for him than for herself. The big head lay upon her breast what time she caressed the gross hair of it ever so lightly. "These are tinsel oaths," she crooned, as rapt with incurious content; "these are but the protestations of a jongleur. A word get you my body? A word get you, in effect, all which you are capable of desiring? Then why do you not speak that word?"

De Gatinais raised clenched hands. "I am shamed," he said; and more lately, "It is just."

He left the room and presently rode away with his men. I say that he had done a knightly deed, but she thought little of it, never raised her head as the troop clattered from Mauleon, with a lessening beat which lapsed now into the blunders of an aging fly who doddered about the pane yonder.

She sat thus for a long period, her meditations adrift in the future; and that which she foreread left her nor all sorry nor profoundly glad, for living seemed by this, though scarcely the merry and colorful business which she had esteemed it, yet immeasurably the more worth while.

THE END OF THE SECOND NOVEL

III

THE STORY OF THE RAT-TRAP

In the year of grace 1298, a little before Candlemas (thus Nicolas begins), came letters to the first King Edward of England from his kinsman and ambassador to France, Earl Edmund of Lancaster. It was perfectly apparent, the Earl wrote, that the French King meant to surrender to the Earl's lord and brother neither the duchy of Guienne nor the Lady Blanch.

The courier found Sire Edward at Ipswich, midway in celebration of his daughter's marriage to the Count of Holland. The King read the letters through and began to laugh; and presently broke into a rage such as was possible to the demon-tainted blood of Anjou. So that next day the keeper of the privy purse entered upon the household-books a considerable sum "to make good a large ruby and an emerald lost out of his coronet when the King's Grace was pleased to throw it into the fire"; and upon the same day the King recalled Lancaster, and more lately despatched yet another embassy into France to treat about Sire Edward's second marriage. This last embassy was headed by the Earl of Aquitaine.

The Earl got audience of the French King at Mezelais. Walking alone came this Earl of Aquitaine, with a large retinue, into the hall where the barons of France stood according to their rank; in russet were the big Earl and his attendants, but upon the scarlets and purples of the French lords many jewels shone; as through a corridor of gayly painted sunlit glass came the grave Earl to the dais where sat King Philippe.

The King had risen at close sight of the new envoy, and had gulped once or twice, and without speaking, hurriedly waved his lords out of ear-shot. His perturbation was very extraordinary.

"Fair cousin," the Earl now said, without any prelude, "four years ago I was affianced to your sister, Dame Blanch. You stipulated that Gascony be given up to you in guaranty, as a settlement on any children I might have by that incomparable lady. I assented, and yielded you the province, upon the understanding, sworn to according to the faith of loyal kings, that within forty days you assign to me its seignory as your vassal. And I have had of you since then neither the enfeoffment nor the lady, but only excuses, Sire Philippe."

With eloquence the Frenchman touched upon the emergencies to which the public weal so often drives men of high station, and upon his private grief over the necessity—unavoidable, alas!—of returning a hard answer before the council; and become so voluble that Sire Edward merely laughed, in that big-lunged and disconcerting way of his, and afterward lodged for a week at Mezelais, nominally passing by his lesser title of Earl of Aquitaine, and as his own ambassador.

And negotiations became more swift of foot, since a man serves himself with zeal. In addition, the French lords could make nothing of a politician so thick-witted that he replied to every consideration of expediency with a parrot-like reiteration of the trivial circumstance that already the bargain was signed and sworn to; and, in consequence, while daily they fumed over his stupidity, daily he gained his point. During this period he was, upon one pretext or another, very largely in the company of his affianced wife, Dame Blanch.

This lady, I must tell you, was the handsomest of her day; there could nowhere be found a creature more agreeable to every sense; and she compelled the eye, it is recorded, not gently but in a superb fashion. And Sire Edward, who, till this, had loved her merely by report, and, in accordance with the high custom of old, through many perusals of her portrait, now appeared besotted. He was an aging man, near sixty; huge and fair he was, with a crisp beard, and stalwart as a tower; and the better-read at Mezelais likened the couple to Sieur Hercules at the feet of Queen Omphale when they saw the two so much together.

The ensuing Wednesday the court hunted and slew a stag of ten in the woods of Ermenoueil, which stand thick about the chateau; and upon that day these two had dined at Rigon the forester's hut, in company with Dame Meregrett, the French King's younger sister. She sat a little apart from the betrothed, and stared through the hut's one window. We know nowadays it was not merely the trees she considered.

Dame Blanch, it seemed, was undisposed to mirth. "For we have slain the stag, beau sire," she said, "and have made of his death a brave diversion. To-day we have had our sport of death,—and presently the gay years wind past us, as our cavalcade came toward the stag, and God's incurious angel slays us, much as we slew the stag. And we will not understand, and we will wonder, as the stag did, in helpless wonder. And Death will have his sport of us, as in atonement." Here her big eyes shone, as the sun glints upon a sand-bottomed pool. "Ohe, I have known such happiness of late, beau sire, that I am hideously afraid

JAMES BRANCH CABELL

to die." And again the heavily fringed eyelids lifted, and within the moment sank contentedly.

For the King had murmured "Happiness!" and his glance was rapacious.

"But I am discourteous," Blanch said, "to prate of death thus drearily. Let us flout him, then, with some gay song." And toward Sire Edward she handed Rigon's lute.

The King accepted it. "Death is not reasonably mocked," Sire Edward said, "since in the end he conquers, and of the very lips that gibed at him remains but a little dust. Nay, rather should I who already stand beneath a lifted sword make for my immediate conqueror a Sirvente, which is the Song of Service."

Sang Sire Edward:

> *I sing of Death, that cometh to the king,*
> *And lightly plucks him from the cushioned throne,*
> *And drowns his glory and his warfaring*
> *In unrecorded dim oblivion,*
> *And girds another with the sword thereof,*
> *And sets another in his stead to reign,*
> *What time the monarch nakedly must gain*
> *Styx' hither shore and nakedly complain*
> *'Midst twittering ghosts lamenting life and love.*
>
> *For Death is merciless: a crack-brained king*
> *He raises in the place of Prester John,*
> *Smites Priam, and mid-course in conquering*
> *Bids Caesar pause; the wit of Salomon,*
> *The wealth of Nero and the pride thereof,*
> *And prowess of great captains—of Gawayne,*
> *Darius, Jeshua, and Charlemaigne—*
> *Wheedle and bribe and surfeit Death in vain*
> *And get no grace of him nor any love.*
>
> *Incuriously he smites the armored king*
> *And tricks his wisest counsellor—*

"True, O God!" murmured the tiny woman, who sat beside the window yonder. And Dame Meregrett rose and in silence passed from the room.

The two started, and laughed in common, and afterward paid little heed to her outgoing. For Sire Edward had put aside the lute and sat now regarding the Princess. His big left hand propped the bearded chin; his grave countenance was flushed, and his intent eyes shone under their shaggy brows, very steadily, like the tapers before an altar.

And, irresolutely, Dame Blanch plucked at her gown; then rearranged a fold of it, and with composure awaited the ensuing action, afraid at bottom, but not at all ill-pleased; and always she looked downward.

The King said: "Never before were we two alone, madame. Fate is very gracious to me this morning."

"Fate," the lady considered, "has never denied much to the Hammer of the Scots."

"She has denied me nothing," he sadly said, "save the one thing that makes this business of living seem a rational proceeding. Fame and power and wealth she has accorded me, no doubt, but never the common joys of life. And, look you, my Princess, I am of aging person now. During some thirty years I have ruled England according to my interpretation of God's will as it was anciently made manifest by the holy Evangelists; and during that period I have ruled England not without odd by-ends of commendation: yet behold, to-day I forget the world-applauded, excellent King Edward, and remember only Edward Plantagenet—hot-blooded and desirous man!—of whom that much-commended king has made a prisoner all these years."

"It is the duty of exalted persons," Blanch unsteadily said, "to put aside such private inclinations as their breasts may harbor—"

He said, "I have done what I might for the happiness of every Englishman within my realm saving only Edward Plantagenet; and now I think his turn to be at hand." Then the man kept silence; and his hot appraisal daunted her.

"Lord," she presently faltered, "lord, in sober verity Love cannot extend his laws between husband and wife, since the gifts of love are voluntary, and husband and wife are but the slaves of duty—"

"Troubadourish nonsense!" Sire Edward said; "yet it is true that the gifts of love are voluntary. And therefore—Ha, most beautiful, what have you and I to do with all this chaffering over Guienne?" The two stood very close to each other now.

Blanch said, "It is a high matter—" Then on a sudden the full-veined girl was aglow with passion. "It is a trivial matter." He took her in his arms, since already her cheeks flared in scarlet anticipation of the event.

JAMES BRANCH CABELL

And thus holding her, he wooed the girl tempestuously. Here, indeed, was Sieur Hercules enslaved, burned by a fiercer fire than that of Nessus, and the huge bulk of the unconquerable visibly shaken by his adoration. In the disordered tapestry of verbiage, passion-flapped as a flag is by the wind, she presently beheld herself prefigured by Balkis, the Judean's lure, and by the Princess of Cyprus (in Aristotle's time), and by Nicolette, the King's daughter of Carthage—since the first flush of morning was as a rush-light before her resplendency, the man swore; and in conclusion, by the Countess of Tripolis, for love of whom he had cleft the seas, and losing whom he must inevitably die as Rudel did. He snapped his fingers now over any consideration of Guienne. He would conquer for her all Muscovy and all Cataia, too, if she desired mere acreage. Meanwhile he wanted her, and his hard and savage passion beat down opposition as with a bludgeon.

"Heart's emperor," the trembling girl more lately said, "I think that you were cast in some larger mould than we of France. Oh, none of us may dare resist you! and I know that nothing matters, nothing in all the world, save that you love me. Then take me, since you will it—and not as King, since you will otherwise, but as Edward Plantagenet. For listen! by good luck you have this afternoon despatched Rigon for Chevrieul, where tomorrow we hunt the great boar. And in consequence to-night this hut will be unoccupied."

The man was silent. He had a gift that way when occasion served.

"Here, then, beau sire! here, then, at nine, you are to meet me with my chaplain. Behold, he marries us, as glibly as though we two were peasants. Poor king and princess!" cried Dame Blanch, and in a voice which thrilled him, "shall ye not, then, dare to be but man and woman?"

"Ha!" the King said. He laughed. "The King is pleased to loose his prisoner; and I will do it." He fiercely said this, for the girl was very beautiful.

So he came that night, without any retinue, and habited as a forester, a horn swung about his neck, into the unlighted hut of Rigon the forester, and found a woman there, though not the woman whom he had perhaps expected.

"Treachery, beau sire! Horrible treachery!" she wailed.

"I have encountered it ere this," the big man said.

"Presently comes not Blanch but Philippe, with many men to back him. And presently they will slay you. You have been trapped, beau sire. Ah, for the love of God, go! Go, while there is yet time!"

Sire Edward reflected. Undoubtedly, to light on Edward Longshanks alone in a forest would appear to King Philippe, if properly attended, a tempting chance to settle divers disputations, once for all; and Sire Edward knew the conscience of his old opponent to be invulnerable. The act would violate all laws of hospitality and knighthood—oh, granted! but its outcome would be a very definite gain to France, and for the rest, merely a dead body in a ditch. Not a monarch in Christendom, Sire Edward reflected, but feared and in consequence hated the Hammer of the Scots, and in further consequence would not lift a finger to avenge him; and not a being in the universe would rejoice at Philippe's achievement one-half so heartily as would Sire Edward's son and immediate successor, the young Prince Edward of Caernarvon. So that, all in all, ohime! Philippe had planned the affair with forethought.

What Sire Edward said was, "Dame Blanch, then, knew of this?" But Meregrett's pitiful eyes had already answered him, and he laughed a little.

"In that event I have to-night enregistered my name among the goodly company of Love's Lunatics—

> *Sots amoureux, sots privez, sots sauvages,*
> *Sots vieux, nouveaux, et sots de tous ages,*

thus he scornfully declaimed, "and as yokefellow with Dan Merlin in his thorn-bush, and with wise Salomon when he capered upon the high places of Chemosh, and with Duke Ares sheepishly agrin within the net of Mulciber. Rogues all, madame! fools all! yet always the flesh trammels us, and allures the soul to such sensual delights as bar its passage toward the eternal life wherein alone lies the empire and the heritage of the soul. And why does this carnal prison so impede the soul? Because Satan once ranked among the sons of God, and the Eternal Father, as I take it, has not yet forgotten the antique relationship—and hence it is permitted even in our late time that always the flesh rebel against the spirit, and always these so tiny and so thin-voiced tricksters, these highly tinted miracles of iniquity, so gracious in demeanor and so starry-eyed—"

Then he turned and pointed, no longer the zealot but the expectant captain now. "Look, my Princess!" For in the pathway from which he had recently emerged stood a man in full armor like a sentinel. "Mort de Dieu, we can but try," Sire Edward said.

"Too late," said Meregrett; and yet she followed him. And presently, in a big splash of moonlight, the armed man's falchion glittered across their way. "Back," he bade them, "for by the King's orders no man passes."

"It were very easy now to strangle this herring," Sire Edward reflected.

"But scarcely a whole school of herring," the fellow retorted. "Nay, Messire d'Aquitaine, the bushes of Ermenoueil are alive with my associates. The hut yonder, in effect, is girdled by them—and we have our orders."

"Concerning women?" the King said.

The man deliberated. Then Sire Edward handed him three gold pieces. "There was assuredly no specific mention of petticoats," the soldier now reflected, "and in consequence I dare to pass the Princess."

"And in that event," Sire Edward said, "we twain had as well bid each other adieu."

But Meregrett only said, "You bid me go?"

He waved his hand. "Since there is no choice. For that which you have done—however tardily—I thank you. Meantime I can but return to Rigon's hut to rearrange my toga as King Caesar did when the assassins fell upon him, and to encounter whatever Dame Luck may send with due decorum."

"To die!" she said.

He shrugged his broad shoulders. "In the end we necessarily die."

Dame Meregrett turned and passed back into the hut without faltering.

And when he had lighted the inefficient lamp which he found there, Sire Edward wheeled upon her in half-humorous vexation. "Presently come your brother and his tattling lords. To be discovered here with me at night, alone, means infamy. If Philippe chance to fall into one of his Capetian rages it means death."

"Nay, lord, it means far worse than death." And she laughed, though not merrily.

And now, for the first time, Sire Edward regarded her with profound consideration, as may we. To the fingertips this so-little lady showed a descendant of the holy Lewis he had known and loved in old years. Small and thinnish she was, with soft and profuse hair that, for all its blackness, gleamed in the lamplight with stray ripples of brilliancy, as you may see a spark shudder to extinction over burning charcoal. The Valois nose she had, long and delicate in form, and overhanging a short upper-lip; yet the lips were glorious in tint, and her skin the very Hyperborean snow in tint. As for her eyes, say, gigantic onyxes—or ebony highly polished and wet with May dew. They were too big for her little face; and they made of her a tiny and desirous wraith which nervously endured each incident of life—invariably acquiescent, as a foreigner must necessarily be, to the custom of the country. In fine, this Meregrett was strange and brightly colored; and she seemed always thrilled with some subtle mirth, like that of a Siren who notes how the sailor pauses at the bulwark and laughs a little (knowing the outcome), and does not greatly care. Yet now Dame Meregrett's countenance was rapt.

And Sire Edward moved one step toward this tiny lady and paused. "Madame, I do not understand."

Dame Meregrett looked up into his face unflinchingly. "It means that I love you, sire. I may speak without shame now, for presently you die. Die bravely, sire! Die in such fashion as may hearten me to live."

The little Princess spoke the truth, for always since his coming to Mezelais she had viewed the great conqueror as through an aweful haze of forerunning rumor, twin to that golden vapor which enswathes a god and transmutes whatever in corporeal man had been a defect into some divine and hitherto unguessed-at excellence. I must tell you in this place, since no other occasion offers, that even until the end of her life it was so. For to her what in other persons would have seemed but flagrant dulness showed, somehow, in Sire Edward, as the majestic deliberation of one that knows his verdict to be decisive, and hence appraises cautiously; and if sometimes his big, calm eyes betrayed no apprehension of the jest at which her lips were laughing, and of which her brain very cordially approved, always within the instant her heart convinced her that a god is not lightly moved to mirth.

And now it was a god—*O deus certe!*—who had taken a woman's paltry face between his hands, half roughly. "And the maid is a Capet!" Sire Edward mused.

"Never has Blanch desired you any ill, beau sire. But it is the Archduke of Austria that she loves, beau sire. And once you were dead, she might marry him. One cannot blame her," Meregrett considered, "since he wishes to marry her, and she, of course, wishes to make him happy."

"And not herself, save in some secondary way!" the big King said. "In part I comprehend, madame. And I, too, long for this same happiness,

JAMES BRANCH CABELL

impotently now, and much as a fevered man might long for water. And my admiration for the Death whom I praised this morning is somewhat abated. There was a Tenson once—Lord, Lord, how long ago! I learn too late that truth may possibly have been upon the losing side—" He took up Rigon's lute.

Sang Sire Edward:

> *Incuriously he smites the armored king*
> *And tricks his wisest counsellor—*

ay, the song ran thus. Now listen, madame—listen, while for me Death waits without, and for you ignominy."

Sang Sire Edward:

> *Anon*
> *Will Death not bid us cease from pleasuring,*
> *And change for idle laughter i' the sun*
> *The grave's long silence and the peace thereof,—*
> *Where we entranced. Death our Viviaine*
> *Implacable, may never more regain*
> *The unforgotten passion, and the pain*
> *And grief and ecstasy of life and love?*
>
> *Yea, presently, as quiet as the king*
> *Sleeps now that laid the walls of Ilion,*
> *We, too, will sleep, and overhead the spring*
> *Laugh, and young lovers laugh—as we have done—*
> *And kiss—as we, that take no heed thereof,*
> *But slumber very soundly, and disdain*
> *The world-wide heralding of winter's wane*
> *And swift sweet ripple of the April rain*
> *Running about the world to waken love.*
>
> *We shall have done with Love, and Death be king*
> *And turn our nimble bodies carrion,*
> *Our red lips dusty;—yet our live lips cling*
> *Spite of that age-long severance and are one*
> *Spite of the grave and the vain grief thereof*
> *We mean to baffle, if in Death's domain*

Old memories may enter, and we twain
May dream a little, and rehearse again
In that unending sleep our present love.

Speed forth to her in sorry unison,
My rhymes: and say Death mocks us, and is slain
Lightly by Love, that lightly thinks thereon;
And that were love at my disposal lain—
All mine to take!—and Death had said, "Refrain,
Lest I demand the bitter cost thereof,"
I know that even as the weather-vane
Follows the wind so would I follow Love.

Sire Edward put aside the lute. "Thus ends the Song of Service," he said, "which was made not by the King of England but by Edward Plantagenet—hot-blooded and desirous man!—in honor of the one woman who within more years than I care to think of has attempted to serve but Edward Plantagenet."

"I do not comprehend," she said. And, indeed, she dared not.

But now he held both tiny hands in his. "At best, your poet is an egotist. I must die presently. Meantime I crave largesse, madame! ay, a great largesse, so that in his unending sleep your poet may rehearse our present love." And even in Rigon's dim light he found her kindling eyes not niggardly.

So that more lately Sire Edward strode to the window and raised big hands toward the spear-points of the aloof stars. "Master of us all!" he cried; "O Father of us all! the Hammer of the Scots am I! the Scourge of France, the conqueror of Llewellyn and of Leicester, and the flail of the accursed race that slew Thine only Son! the King of England am I who have made of England an imperial nation and have given to Thy Englishmen new laws! And to-night I crave my hire. Never, O my Father, have I had of any person aught save reverence or hatred! never in my life has any person loved me! And I am old, my Father—I am old, and presently I die. As I have served Thee— as Jacob wrestled with Thee at the ford of Jabbok—at the place of Peniel—" Against the tremulous blue and silver of the forest she saw in terror how horribly the big man was shaken. "My hire! my hire!" he hoarsely said. "Forty long years, my Father! And now I will not let Thee go except Thou hear me."

JAMES BRANCH CABELL

And presently he turned, stark and black in the rearward splendor of the moon. "*As a prince hast thou power with God*," he calmly said, "*and thou hast prevailed*. For the King of kings was never obdurate, m'amye.

"Child! O brave, brave child!" he said to her a little later, "I was never afraid to die, and yet to-night I would that I might live a trifle longer than in common reason I may ever hope to live!" And their lips met.

Neither stirred when Philippe the Handsome came into the room. At his heels were seven lords, armed cap-a-pie, but the entrance of eight cockchafers had meant as much to these transfigured two.

The French King was an odd man, no more sane, perhaps, than might reasonably be expected of a Valois. Subtly smiling, he came forward through the twilight, with soft, long strides, and made no outcry at recognition of his sister. "Take the woman away; Victor," he said, disinterestedly, to de Montespan. Afterward he sat down beside the table and remained silent for a while, intently regarding Sire Edward and the tiny woman who clung to Sire Edward's arm; and always in the flickering gloom of the hut Philippe smiled as an artist might do who gazes on the perfected work and knows it to be adroit.

"You prefer to remain, my sister?" he presently said. "He bien! it happens that to-night I am in a mood for granting almost any favor. A little later and I will attend to you." The fleet disorder of his visage had lapsed again into the meditative smile which was that of Lucifer watching a toasted soul. "And so it ends," he said. "Conqueror of Scotland, Scourge of France! O unconquerable king! and will the worms of Ermenoueil, then, pause to-morrow to consider through what a glorious turmoil their dinner came to them?"

"You design murder, fair cousin?" Sire Edward said.

The French King shrugged. "I design that within this moment my lords shall slay you while I sit here and do not move a finger. Is it not good to be a king, my cousin, and to sit quite still, and to see your bitterest enemy hacked and slain—and all the while to sit quite still, quite unruffled, as a king should always be? Eh, eh! I never lived until to-night!"

"Now, by Heaven," said Sire Edward, "I am your kinsman and your guest, I am unarmed—"

And Philippe bowed his head. "Undoubtedly," he assented, "the deed is a foul one. But I desire Gascony very earnestly, and so long as you live you will never permit me to retain Gascony. Hence it is quite necessary, you conceive, that I murder you. What!" he presently said, "will you not beg for mercy? I had so hoped," the French King added, somewhat wistfully, "that you might be afraid to die, O huge and righteous man! and would entreat me to spare you. To spurn the weeping conqueror of Llewellyn, say... But these sins which damn one's soul are in actual performance very tedious affairs; and I begin to grow aweary of the game. He bien! now kill this man for me, messieurs."

The English King strode forward. "O shallow trickster!" Sire Edward thundered. *"Am I not afraid?"* You baby, would you ensnare a lion with a flimsy rat-trap? Not so; for it is the nature of a rat-trap, fair cousin, to ensnare not the beast which imperiously desires and takes in daylight, but the tinier and the filthier beast that covets and under darkness pilfers—as you and your seven skulkers!" The man was rather terrible; not a Frenchman within the hut but had drawn back a little.

"Listen!" Sire Edward said, and came yet farther toward the King of France and shook at him one forefinger; "when you were in your cradle I was leading armies. When you were yet unbreeched I was lord of half Europe. For thirty years I have driven kings before me as Fierabras did. Am I, then, a person to be hoodwinked by the first big-bosomed huzzy that elects to waggle her fat shoulders and to grant an assignation in a forest expressively designed for stabbings? You baby, is the Hammer of the Scots the man to trust a Capet? Ill-mannered infant," the King said, with bitter laughter, "it is now necessary that I summon my attendants and remove you to a nursery which I have prepared in England." He set the horn to his lips and blew three blasts.

There came many armed warriors into the hut, bearing ropes. Here was the entire retinue of the Earl of Aquitaine; and, cursing, Sire Philippe sprang upon the English King, and with a dagger smote at the impassive big man's heart. The blade broke against the mail armor under the tunic. "Have I not told you," Sire Edward wearily said, "that one may never trust a Capet? Now, messieurs, bind these carrion and convey them whither I have directed you. Nay, but, Roger—" He conversed apart with his lieutenant, and what Sire Edward commanded was done. The French King and seven lords of France went from that hut trussed like chickens.

And now Sire Edward turned toward Meregrett and chafed his big hands gleefully. "At every tree-bole a tethered horse awaits us; and a ship awaits our party at Fecamp. To-morrow we sleep in England—and, Mort de Dieu! do you not think, madame, that within the Tower your brother and I may more quickly come to some agreement over Guienne?"

She had shrunk from him. "Then the trap was yours? It was you that lured my brother to this infamy!"

"I am vile!" was the man's thought. And, "In effect, I planned it many months ago at Ipswich yonder," Sire Edward gayly said. "Faith of a gentleman! your brother has cheated me of Guienne, and was I to waste an eternity in begging him to restore it? Nay, for I have a many spies in France, and have for some two years known your brother and your sister to the bottom. Granted that I came hither incognito, to forecast your kinfolk's immediate endeavors was none too difficult; and I wanted Guienne—and, in consequence, the person of your brother. Mort de ma vie! Shall not the seasoned hunter adapt his snare aforetime to the qualities of his prey, and take the elephant through his curiosity, as the snake through his notorious treachery?" Now the King of England blustered.

But the little Princess wrung her hands. "I am this night most hideously shamed. Beau sire, I came hither to aid a brave man infamously trapped, and instead I find an alert spider, snug in his cunning web, and patiently waiting until the gnats of France fly near enough. Eh, the greater fool was I to waste my labor on the shrewd and evil thing which has no more need of me than I of it! And now let me go hence, sire, and unmolested, for the sake of chivalry. Could I have come to you but as to the brave man I had dreamed of, I had come through the murkiest lane of hell; as the more artful knave, as the more judicious trickster"—and here she thrust him from her—"I spit upon you. Now let me go hence."

He took her in his brawny arms. "Fit mate for me," he said. "Little vixen, had you done otherwise I had devoted you to the devil."

Anon, still grasping her, and victoriously lifting Dame Meregrett, so that her feet swung quite clear of the floor, Sire Edward said: "Look you, in my time I have played against Fate for considerable stakes—for fortresses, and towns, and strong citadels, and for kingdoms even. And it was only to-night I perceived that the one stake worth playing for is love. It were easy enough to get you for my wife; but I want more than that. . . Pschutt! I know well enough how women have these notions: and carefully I weighed the issue—Meregrett and Guienne to boot? or Meregrett and Meregrett's love to boot?—and thus the final destination of my captives was but the courtyard of Mezelais, in order I might come to you with hands—well! not intolerably soiled."

"Oh, now I love you!" she cried, a-thrill with disappointment. "Yet you have done wrong, for Guienne is a king's ransom."

He smiled whimsically, and presently one arm swept beneath her knees, so that presently he held her as one dandles a baby; and presently his stiff and yellow beard caressed her burning cheek. Masterfully he said: "Then let it serve as such and ransom for a king his glad and common manhood. Ah, m'amye, I am both very wise and abominably selfish. And in either capacity it appears expedient that I leave France without any unwholesome delay. More lately—he, already I have within my pocket the Pope's dispensation permitting me to marry the sister of the King of France, so that I dare to hope."

Very shyly Dame Meregrett lifted her little mouth toward his hot and bearded lips. "Patience," she said, "is a virtue; and daring is a virtue; and hope, too, is a virtue: and otherwise, beau sire, I would not live."

And in consequence, after a deal of political tergiversation (Nicolas concludes), in the year of grace 1299, on the day of our Lady's nativity, and in the twenty-seventh year of King Edward's reign, came to the British realm, and landed at Dover, not Dame Blanch, as would have been in consonance with seasoned expectation, but Dame Meregrett, the other daughter of King Philippe the Bold; and upon the following day proceeded to Canterbury, whither on the next Thursday after came Edward, King of England, into the Church of the Trinity at Canterbury, and therein espoused the aforesaid Dame Meregrett.

THE END OF THE THIRD NOVEL

IV

The Story of the Choices

In the year of grace 1327 (thus Nicolas begins) you could have found in all England no lovers more ardent in affection or in despair more affluent than Rosamund Eastney and Sir Gregory Darrell. She was Lord Berners' only daughter, a brown beauty, and of extensive repute, thanks to such among her retinue of lovers as were practitioners of the Gay Science and had scattered broadcast innumerable Canzons in her honor; and Lord Berners was a man who accepted the world as he found it.

"Dompnedex!" the Earl was wont to say; "in sincerity I am fond of Gregory Darrell, and if he chooses to make love to my daughter that is none of my affair. The eyes and the brain preserve a proverbial warfare, which is the source of all amenity, for without lady-service there would be no songs and tourneys, no measure and no good breeding; and, in a phrase, a man delinquent in it is no more to be valued than an ear of corn without the grain. Nay, I am so profoundly an admirer of Love that I can never willingly behold him slain, of a surfeit, by Matrimony; and besides, the rapscallion could not to advantage exchange purses with Lazarus; and, moreover, Rosamund is to marry the Earl of Sarum a little after All Saints' day."

"Sarum!" people echoed. "Why, the old goat has had two wives already!"

And the Earl would spread his hands. "One of the wealthiest persons in England," he was used to submit.

Thus it fell out that Sir Gregory came and went at his own discretion as concerned Lord Berners' fief of Ordish, all through those gusty times of warfare between Sire Edward and Queen Ysabeau, until at last the Queen had conquered. Lord Berners, for one, vexed himself not inordinately over the outcome of events, since he protested the King's armament to consist of fools and the Queen's of rascals; and had with entire serenity declined to back either Dick or the devil.

It was in the September of this year, a little before Michaelmas, that they brought Sir Gregory Darrell to be judged by the Queen, for notoriously the knight had been Sire Edward's adherent. "Death!"

croaked Adam Orleton, who sat to the right hand, and, "Young de Spencer's death!" amended the Earl of March, with wild laughter; but Ysabeau leaned back in her great chair—a handsome woman, stoutening now from gluttony and from too much wine—and regarded her prisoner with lazy amiability, and devoted the silence to consideration of how scantily the man had changed.

"And what was your errand in Figgis Wood?" she demanded in the ultimate—"or are you mad, then, Gregory Darrell, that you dare ride past my gates alone?"

He curtly said, "I rode for Ordish."

Followed silence. "Roger," the Queen ordered, sharply, "give me the paper which I would not sign."

The Earl of March had drawn an audible breath. The Bishop of London somewhat wrinkled his shaggy brows, as a person in shrewd and epicurean amusement, what while she subscribed the parchment within the moment, with a great scrawling flourish.

"Take, in the devil's name, the hire of your dexterities," said Ysabeau, and pushed this document with her wet pen-point toward March, "and ride for Berkeley now upon that necessary business we know of. And do the rest of you withdraw, saving only my prisoner—my prisoner!" she said, and laughed not very pleasantly.

Followed another silence. Queen Ysabeau lolled in her carven chair, considering the comely gentleman who stood before her, fettered, at the point of shameful death. There was a little dog in the room which had come to the Queen, and now licked the palm of her left hand, and the soft lapping of its tongue was the only sound you heard. "So at peril of your life you rode for Ordish, then, messire?"

The tense man had flushed. "You have harried us of the King's party out of England—and in reason I might not leave England without seeing her."

"My friend," said Ysabeau, as half in sorrow, "I would have pardoned anything save that." She rose. Her face was dark and hot. "By God and all His saints! you shall indeed leave England to-morrow and the world as well! but not without a final glimpse of this same Rosamund. Yet listen: I, too, must ride with you to Ordish—as your sister, say—Gregory, did I not hang last April the husband of your sister? Yes, Ralph de Belomys, a thin man with eager eyes, the Earl of Farrington he was. As his widow will I ride with you to Ordish, upon condition you disclose to none at Ordish, saving only, if you will, this quite immaculate

Rosamund, even a hint of our merry carnival. And to-morrow (you will swear according to the nicest obligations of honor) you must ride back with me to encounter—that which I may devise. For I dare to trust your naked word in this, and, moreover, I shall take with me a sufficiency of retainers to leave you no choice."

Darrell knelt before her. "I can do no homage to Queen Ysabeau; yet the prodigal hands of her who knows that I must die to-morrow and cunningly contrives, for old time's sake, to hearten me with a sight of Rosamund, I cannot but kiss." This much he did. "And I swear in all things to obey her will."

"O comely fool!" the Queen said, not ungently, "I contrive, it may be, but to demonstrate that many tyrants of antiquity were only bunglers. And, besides, I must have other thoughts than that which now occupies my heart: I must this night take holiday, lest I go mad."

Thus did the Queen arrange her holiday.

"Either I mean to torture you to-morrow," Dame Ysabeau said, presently, to Darrell, as these two rode side by side, "or else I mean to free you. In sober verity I do not know. I am in a holiday humor, and it is as the whim may take me. But you indeed do love this Rosamund Eastney? And of course she worships you?"

"It is my belief, madame, that when I see her I tremble visibly, and my weakness is such that a child has more intelligence than I— and toward such misery any lady must in common reason be a little compassionate."

Her hands had twitched so that the astonished palfrey reared. "I design torture," the Queen said; "ah, I perfect exquisite torture, for you have proven recreant, you have forgotten the maid Ysabeau—Le Desir du Cuer, was it not, my Gregory?"

His palms clutched at heaven. "That Ysabeau is dead! and all true joy is destroyed, and the world lies under a blight wherefrom God has averted an unfriendly face in displeasure! yet of all wretched persons existent I am he who endures the most grievous anguish, for daily I partake of life without any relish, and I would in truth deem him austerely kind who slew me now that the maiden Ysabeau is dead."

She shrugged, although but wearily. "I scent the raw stuff of a Planh," the Queen observed; "*benedicite!* it was ever your way, my friend, to love a woman chiefly for the verses she inspired." And she began to sing, as they rode through Baverstock Thicket.

Sang Ysabeau:

Man's love hath many prompters,
But a woman's love hath none;
And he may woo a nimble wit
Or hair that shames the sun,
Whilst she must pick of all one man
And ever brood thereon—
And for no reason,
And not rightly,—

Save that the plan was foreordained
(More old than Chalcedon,
Or any tower of Tarshish
Or of gleaming Babylon),
That she must love unwillingly
And love till life be done,
He for a season,
And more lightly.

So to Ordish in that twilight came the Countess of Farrington, with a retinue of twenty men-at-arms, and her brother Sir Gregory Darrell. Lord Berners received the party with boisterous hospitality.

"And the more for that your sister is a very handsome woman," was Rosamund Eastney's comment. The period appears to have been after supper, and she sat with Gregory Darrell in not the most brilliant corner of the main hall.

The wretched man leaned forward, bit his nether-lip, and then with a sudden splurge of speech informed her of the sorry masquerade. "The she-devil designs some horrible and obscure mischief, she plans I know not what."

"Yet I—" said Rosamund. The girl had risen, and she continued with an odd inconsequence. "You have told me you were Pembroke's squire when long ago he sailed for France to fetch this woman into England—"

"Which you never heard!" Lord Berners shouted at this point. "Jasper, a lute!" And then he halloaed, more lately, "Gregory, Madame de Farrington demands that racy song you made against Queen Ysabeau during your last visit."

Thus did the Queen begin her holiday.

It was a handsome couple which came forward, hand quitting hand a shade too tardily, and the blinking eyes yet rapt; but these two were not overpleased at being disturbed, and the man in particular was troubled, as in reason he well might be, by the task assigned him.

"Is it, indeed, your will, my sister," he said, "that I should sing—this song?"

"It is my will," the Countess said.

And the knight flung back his comely head and laughed. "What I have written I shall not disown in any company. It is not, look you, of my own choice that I sing, my sister. Yet if she bade me would I sing this song as willingly before Queen Ysabeau, for, Christ aid me! the song is true."

Sang Sir Gregory:

> *Dame Ysabeau, la prophecie*
> *Que li sage dit ne ment mie,*
> *Que la royne sut ceus grever*
> *Qui tantost laquais sot aymer—*

and so on. It was a lengthy ditty and in its wording not oversqueamish; the Queen's career in England was detailed without any stuttering, and you would have found the catalogue unhandsome. Yet Sir Gregory sang it with an incisive gusto, though it seemed to him to countersign his death-warrant; and with the vigor that a mangled snake summons for its last hideous stroke, it seemed to Ysabeau regretful of an ancient spring.

Nicolas gives this ballad in full, but, and for obvious reasons, his translator would prefer to do otherwise.

Only the minstrel added, though Lord Berners did not notice it, a fire-new peroration.

Sang Sir Gregory:

> *Ma voix mocque, mon cuer gemit—*
> *Peu pense a ce que la voix dit,*
> *Car me membre du temps jadis*
> *Et d'ung garson, d'amour surpris,*
> *Et d'une fille—et la vois si—*
> *Et grandement suis esbahi.*

And when Darrell had ended, the Countess of Farrington, without speaking, swept her left hand toward her cheek and by pure chance caught between thumb and forefinger the autumn-numbed fly that had annoyed her. She drew the little dagger from her girdle and meditatively cut the buzzing thing in two. Then she flung the fragments from her, and resting the dagger's point upon the arm of her chair, one forefinger upon the summit of the hilt, considerately twirled the brilliant weapon.

"This song does not err upon the side of clemency," she said at last, "nor by ordinary does Queen Ysabeau."

"That she-wolf!" said Lord Berners, comfortably. "Hoo, Madame Gertrude! since the Prophet Moses wrung healing waters from a rock there has been no such miracle recorded."

"We read, Messire de Berners, that when the she-wolf once acknowledges a master she will follow him as faithfully as any dog. Nay, my brother, I do not question your sincerity, yet you sing with the voice of an unhonored courtier. Suppose Queen Ysabeau had heard your song all through and then had said—for she is not as the run of women— 'Messire, I had thought till this there was no thorough man in England saving Roger Mortimer. I find him tawdry now, and—I remember. Come you, then, and rule the England that you love as you may love no woman, and rule me, messire, for I find even in your cruelty—England! bah, we are no pygmies, you and I!'" the Countess said with a great voice; "'yonder is squabbling Europe and all the ancient gold of Africa, ready for our taking! and past that lies Asia, too, and its painted houses hung with bells, and cloud-wrapt Tartary, wherein we twain may yet erect our equal thrones, whereon to receive the tributary emperors! For we are no pygmies, you and I.'" She paused and more lately shrugged. "Suppose Queen Ysabeau had said this much, my brother?"

Darrell was more pallid, as the phrase is, than a sheet, and the lute had dropped unheeded, and his hands were clenched.

"I would answer, my sister, that as she has found in England but one man, I have found in England but one woman—the rose of all the world." His eyes were turned at this toward Rosamund Eastney. "And yet," the man stammered, "for that I, too, remember—"

"Nay, in God's name! I am answered," the Countess said. She rose, in dignity almost a queen. "We have ridden far to-day, and to-morrow we must travel a deal farther—eh, my brother? I am a trifle overspent, Messire de Berners." And her face had now the weary beauty of an idol's.

So the men and women parted. Madame de Farrington kissed her brother in leaving him, as was natural; and under her caress his stalwart person shuddered, but not in repugnance; and the Queen went bedward regretful of an ancient spring and singing hushedly.

Sang Ysabeau:

> *Were the All-Mother wise, life (shaped anotherwise)*
> *Would be all high and true;*
> *Could I be otherwise I had been otherwise*
> *Simply because of you,*
> *Who are no longer you.*

> *Life with its pay to be bade us essay to be*
> *What we became,—I believe*
> *Were there a way to be what it was play to be*
> *I would not greatly grieve. . .*
> *And I neither laugh nor grieve!*

Ysabeau would have slept that night within the chamber of Rosamund Eastney had either slept at all. As concerns the older I say nothing. The girl, though soon aware of frequent rustlings near at hand, lay quiet, half-forgetful of the poisonous woman yonder. The girl was now fulfilled with a great blaze of exultation; to-morrow Gregory must die, and then perhaps she might find time for tears; but meanwhile, before her eyes, the man had flung away a kingdom and life itself for love of her, and the least nook of her heart ached to be a shade more worthy of the sacrifice.

After it might have been an hour of this excruciate ecstasy the Countess came to Rosamund's bed. "Ay," the woman hollowly began, "it is indisputable that his hair is like spun gold and that his eyes resemble sun-drenched waters in June. And that when this Gregory laughs God is more happy. Ma belle, I was familiar with the routine of your meditations ere you were born."

Rosamund said, quite simply: "You have known him always. I envy the circumstance, Madame Gertrude—you alone of all women in the world I envy, since you, his sister, being so much older, must have known him always."

"I know him to the core, my girl," the Countess answered, and afterward sat silent, one bare foot jogging restlessly; "yet am I two years the junior—Did you hear nothing, Rosamund?"

"Nay, Madame Gertrude, I heard nothing."

"Strange!" the Countess said; "let us have lights, since I can no longer endure the overpopulous darkness." She kindled, with twitching fingers, three lamps and looked in vain for more. "It is as yet dark yonder, where the shadows quiver very oddly, as though they would rise from the floor—do they not, my girl?—and protest vain things. Nay, Rosamund, it has been done; in the moment of death men's souls have travelled farther and have been visible; it has been done, I tell you. And he would stand before me, with pleading eyes, and reproach me in a voice too faint to reach my ears—but I would see him—and his groping hands would clutch at my hands as though a dropped veil had touched me, and with the contact I would go mad!"

"Madame Gertrude!" the girl now stammered, in communicated terror.

"Poor innocent dastard!" the woman said, "I am Ysabeau of France." And when Rosamund made as though to rise, in alarm, Queen Ysabeau caught her by the shoulder. "Bear witness when he comes I never hated him. Yet for my quiet it was necessary that it suffer so cruelly, the scented, pampered body, and no mark be left upon it! Eia! even now he suffers! Nay, I have lied. I hate the man, and in such fashion as you will comprehend only when you are Sarum's wife."

"Madame and Queen!" the girl said, "you will not murder me!"

"I am tempted!" the Queen hissed. "O little slip of girlhood, I am tempted, for it is not reasonable you should possess everything that I have lost. Innocence you have, and youth, and untroubled eyes, and quiet dreams, and the glad beauty of the devil, and Gregory Darrell's love—" Now Ysabeau sat down upon the bed and caught up the girl's face between two fevered hands. "Rosamund, this Darrell perceives within the moment, as I do, that the love he bears for you is but what he remembers of the love he bore a certain maid long dead. Eh, you might have been her sister, Rosamund, for you are very like her. And she, poor wench—why, I could see her now, I think, were my eyes not blurred, somehow, almost as though Queen Ysabeau might weep! But she was handsomer than you, since your complexion is not overclear, praise God!"

Woman against woman they were. "He has told me of his intercourse with you," the girl said, and this was a lie flatfooted. "Nay, kill me if you will, madame, since you are the stronger, yet, with my dying breath, Gregory has loved but me."

"Ma belle," the Queen answered, and laughed bitterly, "do I not know men? He told you nothing. And to-night he hesitated, and to-morrow,

JAMES BRANCH CABELL

at the lifting of my finger, he will supplicate. Throughout his life has Gregory Darrell loved me, O white, palsied innocence! and he is mine at a whistle. And in that time to come he will desert you, Rosamund— though with a pleasing Canzon—and they will give you to the gross Earl of Sarum, as they gave me to the painted man who was of late our King! and in that time to come you will know your body to be your husband's makeshift when he lacks leisure to seek out other recreation! and in that time to come you will long at first for death, and presently your heart will be a flame within you, my Rosamund, an insatiable flame! and you will hate your God because He made you, and hate Satan because in some desperate hour he tricked you, and hate all masculinity because, poor fools, they scurry to obey your whim! and chiefly hate yourself because you are so pitiable! and devastation only will you love in that strange time which is to come. It is adjacent, my Rosamund."

The girl kept silence. She sat erect in the tumbled bed, her hands clasping her knees, and appeared to deliberate what Dame Ysabeau had said. The plentiful brown hair fell about this Rosamund's face, which was white and shrewd. "A part of what you say, madame, I understand. I know that Gregory Darrell loves me, yet I have long ago acknowledged he loves me but as one pets a child, or, let us say, a spaniel which reveres and amuses one. I lack his wit, you comprehend, and so he never speaks to me all that he thinks. Yet a part of it he tells me, and he loves me, and with this I am content. Assuredly, if they give me to Sarum I shall hate Sarum even more than I detest him now. And then, I think, Heaven help me! that I would not greatly grieve—Oh, you are all evil!" Rosamund said; "and you thrust thoughts into my mind I may not grapple with!"

"You will comprehend them," the Queen said, "when you know yourself a chattel, bought and paid for."

The Queen laughed. She rose, and either hand strained toward heaven. "You are omnipotent, yet have You let me become that into which I am transmuted," she said, very low.

Anon she began, as though a statue spoke through motionless and pallid lips. "They have long urged me, Rosamund, to a deed which by one stroke would make me mistress of these islands. To-day I looked on Gregory Darrell, and knew that I was wise in love—and I had but to crush a filthy worm to come to him. Eh, and I was tempted—!"

The fearless girl said: "Let us grant that Gregory loves you very greatly, and me just when his leisure serves. You may offer him a cushioned infamy, a colorful and brief delirium, and afterward demolishment of soul and body; I offer him contentment and a level life, made up of tiny happenings, it may be, and lacking both in abysses and in skyey heights. Yet is love a flame wherein must the lover's soul be purified, as an ore by fire, even to its own discredit; and thus, madame, to judge between us I dare summon you."

"Child, child!" the Queen said, tenderly, and with a smile, "you are brave; and in your fashion you are wise; yet you will never comprehend. But once I was in heart and soul and body all that you are to-day; and now I am Queen Ysabeau. Assuredly, it would be hard to yield my single chance of happiness; it would be hard to know that Gregory Darrell must presently dwindle into an ox well-pastured, and garner of life no more than any ox; but to say, 'Let this girl become as I, and garner that which I have garnered—!' Did you in truth hear nothing, Rosamund?"

"Why, nothing save the wind."

"Strange!" said the Queen; "since all the while that I have talked with you I have been seriously annoyed by shrieks and various imprecations! But I, too, grow cowardly, it maybe—Nay, I know," she said, and in a resonant voice, "that I am by this mistress of broad England, until my son—my own son, born of my body, and in glad anguish, Rosamund—knows me for what I am. For I have heard—Coward! O beautiful sleek coward!" the Queen said; "I would have died without lamentation and I was but your plaything!"

"Madame Ysabeau—!" the girl stammered, and ran toward her, for the girl had risen, and she was terrified.

"To bed!" said Ysabeau; "and put out the lights lest he come presently. Or perhaps he fears me now too much to come to-night. Yet the night approaches, none the less, when I must lift some arras and find him there, chalk-white, with painted cheeks, and rigid, and smiling very terribly, or look into some mirror and behold there not myself but him—and in that instant I will die. Meantime I rule, until my son attains his manhood. Eh, Rosamund, my only son was once so tiny, and so helpless, and his little crimson mouth groped toward me, helplessly, and save in Bethlehem, I thought, there was never any child more fair—But I must forget all that, for even now he plots. Hey, God orders matters very shrewdly, my Rosamund."

And timidly the girl touched one shoulder. "In part, I understand, madame and Queen."

"You understand nothing," said Ysabeau; "how should you understand whose breasts are yet so tiny? Nay, put out the light! though I dread the darkness, Rosamund—For they say that hell is poorly lighted—and they say—" Then Queen Ysabeau shrugged. Herself blew out each lamp.

"We know this Gregory Darrell," the Queen said in the darkness, and aloud, "ay, to the marrow we know him, however steadfastly we blink, and we know the present turmoil of his soul; and in common-sense what chance have you of victory?"

"None in common-sense, madame, and yet you go too fast. For man is a being of mingled nature, we are told by those in holy orders, and his life here but one unending warfare between that which is divine in him and that which is bestial, while impartial Heaven attends as arbiter of the cruel tourney. Always his judgment misleads the man, and his faculties allure him to a truce, however brief, with iniquity. His senses raise a mist about his goings, and there is not an endowment of the man but in the end plays traitor to his interest, as of His wisdom God intends; so that when the man is overthrown, God the Eternal Father may, in reason, be neither vexed nor grieved if only he takes heart to rise again. And when, betrayed and impotent, the man elects to fight out the allotted battle, defiant of common-sense and of the counsellors which God Himself accorded, I think that they hold festival in heaven."

"A very pretty sermon," said the Queen, and with premeditation yawned.

Followed a silence, vexed only on the purposeless September winds; but I believe that neither of these two slept with an inappropriate profundity.

About dawn one of the Queen's attendants roused Sir Gregory Darrell and presently conducted him into the hedged garden of Ordish, where Ysabeau walked in tranquil converse with Lord Berners. The old man was in high good-humor.

"My lad," said he, and clapped Sir Gregory upon the shoulder, "you have, I do protest, the very phoenix of sisters. I was never happier." And he went away chuckling.

The Queen said in a toneless voice, "We ride for Blackfriars now."

Darrell responded, "I am content, and ask but leave to speak, and briefly, with Dame Rosamund before I die."

Then the woman came more near to him. "I am not used to beg, but within this hour you die, and I have loved no man in all my life saving only you, Sir Gregory Darrell. Nor have you loved any person as you loved me once in France. Nay, to-day, I may speak freely, for with you the doings of that boy and girl are matters overpast. Yet were it otherwise—eh, weigh the matter carefully! for absolute mistress of England am I now, and entire England would I give you, and such love as that slim, white innocence has never dreamed of would I give you, Gregory Darrell—No, no! ah, Mother of God, not you!" The Queen clapped one hand upon his lips.

"Listen," she quickly said, as a person in the crisis of panic; "I spoke to tempt you. But you saw, and clearly, that it was the sickly whim of a wanton, and you never dreamed of yielding, for you love this Rosamund Eastney, and you know me to be vile. Then have a care of me! The strange woman am I of whom we read that her house is the way to hell, going down to the chambers of death. Yea, many strong men have been slain by me, and futurely will many others be slain, it may be; but never you among them, my Gregory, who are more wary, and more merciful, and know that I have need to lay aside at least one comfortable thought against eternity."

"I concede you to have been unwise—" he hoarsely said.

About them fell the dying leaves, of many glorious colors, but the air of this new day seemed raw and chill.

Then Rosamund came through the opening in the hedge. "Nay, choose," she wearily said; "the woman offers life and empery and wealth, and it may be, even a greater love than I am capable of giving you. I offer a dishonorable death within the moment."

And again, with that peculiar and imperious gesture, the man flung back his head, and he laughed. "I am I! and I will so to live that I may face without shame not only God, but even my own scrutiny." He wheeled upon the Queen and spoke henceforward very leisurely. "I love you; all my life long I have loved you, Ysabeau, and even now I love you: and you, too, dear Rosamund, I love, though with a difference. And every fibre of my being lusts for the power that you would give me, Ysabeau, and for the good which I would do with it in the England I or Roger Mortimer must rule; as every fibre of my being lusts for the man that I would be could I choose death without debate, and for the man which you would make of me, my Rosamund.

"The man! And what is this man, this Gregory Darrell, that his welfare be considered?—an ape who chatters to himself of kinship with the archangels while filthily he digs for groundnuts! This much I know, at bottom, durst I but be honest.

JAMES BRANCH CABELL

"Yet more clearly do I perceive that this same man, like all his fellows, is a maimed god who walks the world dependent upon many wise and evil counsellors. He must measure, and to a hair's-breadth, every content of the world by means of a bloodied sponge, tucked somewhere in his skull, which is ungeared by the first cup of wine and ruined by the touch of his own finger. He must appraise all that he judges with no better instruments than two bits of colored jelly, with a bungling makeshift so maladroit that the nearest horologer's apprentice could have devised a more accurate device. In fine, he is under penalty condemned to compute eternity with false weights and to estimate infinity with a yardstick: and he very often does it. For though, 'If then I do that which I would not I consent unto the law,' saith even the Apostle; yet the braver Pagan answers him, 'Perceive at last that thou hast in thee something better and more divine than the things which cause the various effects and, as it were, pull thee by the strings.'

"There lies the choice which every man must make—or rationally, as his reason goes, to accept his own limitations and make the best of his allotted prison-yard? or stupendously to play the fool and swear even to himself (while his own judgment shrieks and proves a flat denial), that he is at will omnipotent? You have chosen long ago, my poor proud Ysabeau; and I choose now, and differently: for poltroon that I am! being now in a cold drench of terror, I steadfastly protest I am not much afraid, and I choose death, madame."

It was toward Rosamund that the Queen looked, and smiled a little pitifully. "Should Queen Ysabeau be angry or vexed or very cruel now, my Rosamund? for at bottom she is glad."

More lately the Queen said: "I give you back your plighted word. I ride homeward to my husks, but you remain. Or rather, the Countess of Farrington departs for the convent of Ambresbury, disconsolate in her widowhood and desirous to have done with worldly affairs. It is most natural she should relinquish to her beloved and only brother all her dower-lands—or so at least Messire de Berners acknowledges. Here, then, is the grant, my Gregory, that conveys to you those lands of Ralph de Belomys which last year I confiscated. And this tedious Messire de Berners is willing now—nay, desirous—to have you for a son-in-law."

About them fell the dying leaves, of many glorious colors, but the air of this new day seemed raw and chill, what while, very calmly, Dame Ysabeau took Sir Gregory's hand and laid it upon the hand of Rosamund Eastney. "Our paladin is, in the outcome, a mortal man, and therefore I do not altogether envy you. Yet he has his moments, and you are capable. Serve, then, not only his desires but mine also, dear Rosamund."

There was a silence. The girl spoke as though it was a sacrament. "I will, madame and Queen."

Thus did the Queen end her holiday.

A little later the Countess of Farrington rode from Ordish with all her train save one; and riding from that place, where love was, she sang very softly, and as to herself.

Sang Ysabeau:

> *As with her dupes dealt Circe*
> *Life deals with hers, pardie!*
> *Reshaping without mercy,*
> *And shaping swinishly,*
> *To wallow swinishly,*
> *And for eternity—*
>
> *Though, harder than the witch was,*
> *Life, changing ne'er the whole,*
> *Transmutes the body, which was*
> *Proud garment of the soul,*
> *And briefly drugs the soul,*
> *Whose ruin is her goal—*
>
> *And means by this thereafter*
> *A subtler mirth to get,*
> *And mock with bitterer laughter*
> *Her helpless dupes' regret,*
> *Their swinish dull regret*
> *For what they half forget.*

And within the hour came Hubert Frayne to Ordish, on a foam-specked horse, as he rode to announce to the King's men the King's barbaric murder overnight, at Berkeley Castle, by Queen Ysabeau's order.

"Ride southward," said Lord Berners, and panted as they buckled on his disused armor; "but harkee, Frayne! if you pass the Countess of Farrington's company, speak no syllable of your news, since it is not convenient that a lady so thoroughly and so praiseworthily—Lord,

Lord, how I have fattened!—so intent on holy things, in fine, should have her meditations disturbed by any such unsettling tidings. Hey, son-in-law?"

Sir Gregory Darrell laughed, and very bitterly. "He that is without blemish among you—" he said. Then they armed completely.

THE END OF THE FOURTH NOVEL

V

THE STORY OF THE HOUSEWIFE

In the year of grace 1326, upon Walburga's Eve, some three hours after sunset (thus Nicolas begins), had you visited a certain garden on the outskirts of Valenciennes, you might there have stumbled upon a big, handsome boy, prone on the turf, where by turns he groaned and vented himself in sullen curses. The profanity had its poor palliation. Heir to England though he was, you must know that his father in the flesh had hounded him from England, as more recently his uncle Charles the Handsome had driven him from France. Now had this boy's mother and he come as suppliants to the court of that stalwart nobleman Sire William (Count of Hainault, Holland, and Zealand, and Lord of Friesland), where their arrival had evoked the suggestion that they depart at their earliest convenience. To-morrow, then, these footsore royalties, the Queen of England and the Prince of Wales, would be thrust out-o'-doors to resume the weary beggarship, to knock again upon the obdurate gates of this unsympathizing king or that deaf emperor.

Accordingly the boy aspersed his destiny. At hand a nightingale carolled as though an exiled prince were the blithest spectacle the moon knew.

There came through the garden a tall girl, running, stumbling in her haste. "Hail, King of England!" she panted.

"Do not mock me, Philippa!" the boy half-sobbed. Sulkily he rose to his feet.

"No mockery here, my fair sweet friend. Nay, I have told my father all which happened yesterday. I pleaded for you. He questioned me very closely. And when I had ended, he stroked his beard, and presently struck one hand upon the table. 'Out of the mouth of babes!' he said. Then he said: 'My dear, I believe for certain that this lady and her son have been driven from their kingdom wrongfully. If it be for the good of God to comfort the afflicted, how much more is it commendable to help and succor one who is the daughter of a king, descended from royal lineage, and to whose blood we ourselves are related!' And accordingly he and your mother have their heads together yonder, planning an invasion of England, no less, and the dethronement of your wicked father, my Edward. And accordingly—hail, King of England!" The girl clapped her hands gleefully, what time the nightingale sang on.

But the boy kept momentary silence. Even in youth the Plantagenets were never handicapped by excessively tender hearts; yesterday in the shrubbery the boy had kissed this daughter of Count William, in part because she was a healthy and handsome person, and partly, and with consciousness of the fact, as a necessitated hazard of futurity. Well! he had found chance-taking not unfortunate. With the episode as foundation, Count William had already builded up the future queenship of England. A wealthy count could do—and, as it seemed, was now in train to do—indomitable deeds to serve his son-in-law; and now the beggar of five minutes since foresaw himself, with this girl's love as ladder, mounting to the high habitations of the King of England, the Lord of Ireland, and the Duke of Aquitaine. Thus they would herald him.

So he embraced the girl. "Hail, Queen of England!" said the Prince; and then, "If I forget—" His voice broke awkwardly. "My dear, if ever I forget—!" Their lips met now, what time the nightingale discoursed as on a wager.

Presently was mingled with the bird's descant low singing of another kind. Beyond the yew-hedge as these two stood silent, breast to breast, passed young Jehan Kuypelant, the Brabant page, fitting to the accompaniment of a lute his paraphrase of the song which Archilochus of Sicyon very anciently made in honor of Venus Melaenis, the tender Venus of the Dark.

At a gap in the hedge the Brabanter paused. His melody was hastily gulped. You saw, while these two stood heart hammering against heart, his lean face silvered by the moonlight, his mouth a tiny abyss. Followed the beat of lessening footsteps, while the nightingale improvised his envoi.

But earlier Jehan Kuypelant also had sung, as though in rivalry with the bird.

Sang Jehan Kuypelant:

> *Hearken and heed, Melaenis!*
> *For all that the litany ceased*
> *When Time had taken the victim,*
> *And flouted thy pale-lipped priest,*
> *And set astir in the temple*
> *Where burned the fire of thy shrine*

The owls and wolves of the desert—
Yet hearken, (the issue is thine!)
And let the heart of Atys,
At last, at last, be mine!

For I have followed, nor faltered—
Adrift in a land of dreams
Where laughter and loving and wonder
Contend as a clamor of streams,
I have seen and adored the Sidonian,
Implacable, fair and divine—
And bending low, have implored thee
To hearken, (the issue is thine!)
And let the heart of Atys,
At last, at last, be mine!

It is time, however, that we quit this subject and speak of other matters. Just twenty years later, on one August day in the year of grace 1346, Master John Copeland—as men now called the Brabant page, now secretary to the Queen of England—brought his mistress the unhandsome tidings that David Bruce had invaded her realm with forty thousand Scots to back him. The Brabanter found the Queen in company with the kingdom's arbitress—Dame Catherine de Salisbury, whom King Edward, third of that name to reign in Britain, and now warring in France, very notoriously adored and obeyed.

This king, indeed, had been despatched into France chiefly, they narrate, to release the Countess' husband, William de Montacute, from the French prison of the Chatelet. You may appraise her dominion by this fact: chaste and shrewd, she had denied all to King Edward, and in consequence he could deny her nothing; so she sent him to fetch back her husband, whom she almost loved. That armament had sailed from Southampton on Saint George's day.

These two women, then, shared the Brabanter's execrable news. Already Northumberland, Westmoreland, and Durham were the broken meats of King David.

The Countess presently exclaimed: "Let me pass, sir! My place is not here."

Philippa said, half hopefully, "Do you forsake Sire Edward, Catherine?"

"Madame and Queen," the Countess answered, "in this world every man must scratch his own back. My lord has entrusted to me his castle of Wark, his fiefs in Northumberland. These, I hear, are being laid waste. Were there a thousand men-at-arms left in England I would say fight. As it is, our men are yonder in France and the island is defenceless. Accordingly I ride for the north to make what terms I may with the King of Scots."

Now you might have seen the Queen's eyes flame. "Undoubtedly," said she, "in her lord's absence it is the wife's part to defend his belongings. And my lord's fief is England. I bid you God-speed, Catherine." And when the Countess was gone, Philippa turned, her round face all flushed. "She betrays him! she compounds with the Scot! Mother of Christ, let me not fail!"

"A ship must be despatched to bid Sire Edward return," said the secretary. "Otherwise all England is lost."

"Not so, John Copeland! Let Sire Edward conquer in France, if such be the Trinity's will. Always he has dreamed of that, and if I bade him return now he would be vexed."

"The disappointment of the King," John Copeland considered, "is a lesser evil than allowing all of us to be butchered."

"Not to me, John Copeland," the Queen said.

Now came many lords into the chamber, seeking Madame Philippa. "We must make peace with the Scottish rascal!—England is lost!—A ship must be sent entreating succor of Sire Edward!" So they shouted.

"Messieurs," said Queen Philippa, "who commands here? Am I, then, some woman of the town?"

Ensued a sudden silence. John Copeland, standing by the seaward window, had picked up a lute and was fingering the instrument half-idly. Now the Marquess of Hastings stepped from the throng. "Pardon, Highness. But the occasion is urgent."

"The occasion is very urgent, my lord," the Queen assented, deep in meditation.

John Copeland flung back his head and without prelude began to carol lustily.

Sang John Copeland:

> *There are fairer men than Atys,*
> *And many are wiser than he—*
> *How should I heed them?—whose fate is*
> *Ever to serve and to be*

Ever the lover of Atys,
And die that Atys may dine,
Live if he need me—Then heed me,
And speed me, (the moment is thine!)
And let the heart of Atys,
At last, at last, be mine!

Fair is the form unbeholden,
And golden the glory of thee
Whose voice is the voice of a vision,
Whose face is the foam of the sea,
And the fall of whose feet is the flutter
Of breezes in birches and pine,
When thou drawest near me, to hear me,
And cheer me, (the moment is thine!)
And let the heart of Atys,
At last, at last, be mine!

I must tell you that the Queen shivered, as with extreme cold. She gazed toward John Copeland wonderingly. The secretary was as of stone, fretting at his lute-strings, head downcast. Then in a while the Queen turned to Hastings.

"The occasion is very urgent, my lord," the Queen assented. "Therefore it is my will that to-morrow one and all your men be mustered at Blackheath. We will take the field without delay against the King of Scots."

The riot began anew. "Madness!" they shouted; "lunar madness! We can do nothing until the King return with our army!"

"In his absence," the Queen said, "I command here."

"You are not Regent," the Marquess said. Then he cried, "This is the Regent's affair!"

"Let the Regent be fetched," Dame Philippa said, very quietly. Presently they brought in her son, Messire Lionel, now a boy of eight years, and Regent, in name at least, of England.

Both the Queen and the Marquess held papers. "Highness," Lord Hastings began, "for reasons of state, which I need not here explain, this document requires your signature. It is an order that a ship be despatched in pursuit of the King. Your Highness may remember the pony you admired yesterday?" The Marquess smiled ingratiatingly. "Just here, your Highness—a cross-mark."

"The dappled one?" said the Regent; "and all for making a little mark?" The boy jumped for the pen.

"Lionel," said the Queen, "you are Regent of England, but you are also my son. If you sign that paper you will beyond doubt get the pony, but you will not, I think, care to ride him. You will not care to sit down at all, Lionel."

The Regent considered. "Thank you very much, my lord," he said in the ultimate, "but I do not like ponies any more. Do I sign here, mother?"

Philippa handed the Marquess a subscribed order to muster the English forces at Blackheath; then another, closing the English ports. "My lords," the Queen said, "this boy is the King's vicar. In defying him, you defy the King. Yes, Lionel, you have fairly earned a pot of jam for supper."

Then Hastings went away without speaking. That night assembled at his lodgings, by appointment, Viscount Heringaud, Adam Frere, the Marquess of Orme, Lord Stourton, the Earls of Neville and Gage, and Sir Thomas Rokeby. These seven found a long table there littered with pens and parchment; to the rear of it, a lackey behind him, sat the Marquess of Hastings, meditative over a cup of Bordeaux.

Presently Hastings said: "My friends, in creating our womankind the Maker of us all was beyond doubt actuated by laudable and cogent reasons; so that I can merely lament my inability to fathom these reasons. I shall obey the Queen faithfully, since if I did otherwise Sire Edward would have my head off within a day of his return. In consequence, I do not consider it convenient to oppose his vicar. To-morrow I shall assemble the tatters of troops which remain to us, and to-morrow we march northward to inevitable defeat. To-night I am sending a courier into Northumberland. He is an obliging person, and would convey—to cite an instance—eight letters quite as blithely as one."

Each man glanced furtively about him. England was in a panic by this, and knew itself to lie before the Bruce defenceless. The all-powerful Countess of Salisbury had compounded with King David; now Hastings too, their generalissimo, compounded. What the devil! loyalty was a sonorous word, and so was patriotism, but, after all, one had estates in the north.

The seven wrote in silence. When they had ended, I must tell you that Hastings gathered the letters into a heap, and without glancing at the superscriptures, handed all these letters to the attendant lackey. "For the courier," he said.

The fellow left the apartment. Presently there was a clatter of hoofs without, and Hastings rose. He was a gaunt, terrible old man, gray-bearded, and having high eyebrows that twitched and jerked.

"We have saved our precious skins," said he. "Hey, you Iscariots! I commend your common-sense, messieurs, and I request you to withdraw. Even a damned rogue such as I has need of a cleaner atmosphere when he would breathe." The seven went away without further speech.

They narrate that next day the troops marched for Durham, where the Queen took up her quarters. The Bruce had pillaged and burned his way to a place called Beaurepair, within three miles of the city. He sent word to the Queen that if her men were willing to come forth from the town he would abide and give them battle.

She replied that she accepted his offer, and that the barons would gladly risk their lives for the realm of their lord the King. The Bruce grinned and kept silence, since he had in his pocket letters from nine-tenths of them protesting they would do nothing of the sort.

There is comedy here. On one side you have a horde of half-naked savages, a shrewd master holding them in leash till the moment be auspicious; on the other, a housewife at the head of a tiny force lieutenanted by perjurers, by men already purchased. God knows the dreams she had of miraculous victories, what time her barons trafficked in secret with the Bruce. On the Saturday before Michaelmas, when the opposing armies marshalled in the Bishop's Park, at Auckland, it is recorded that not a captain on either side believed the day to be pregnant with battle. There would be a decent counterfeit of resistance; afterward the little English army would vanish pell-mell, and the Bruce would be master of the island. The farce was prearranged, the actors therein were letter-perfect.

That morning at daybreak John Copeland came to the Queen's tent, and informed her quite explicitly how matters stood. He had been drinking overnight with Adam Frere and the Earl of Gage, and after the third bottle had found them candid. "Madame and Queen, we are betrayed. The Marquess of Hastings, our commander, is inexplicably smitten with a fever. He will not fight to-day. Not one of your lords will fight to-day." Master Copeland laid bare such part of the scheme as yesterday's conviviality had made familiar. "Therefore I counsel retreat. Let the King be summoned out of France."

But Queen Philippa shook her head, as she cut up squares of toast and dipped them in milk for the Regent's breakfast. "Sire Edward would be vexed. He has always intended to conquer France. I shall visit

JAMES BRANCH CABELL

the Marquess as soon as Lionel is fed—do you know, John Copeland, I am anxious about Lionel; he is irritable and coughed five times during the night—and then I will attend to this affair."

She found the Marquess in bed, groaning, the coverlet pulled up to his chin. "Pardon, Highness," said Lord Hastings, "but I am an ill man. I cannot rise from this couch."

"I do not question the gravity of your disorder," the Queen retorted, "since it is well known that the same illness brought about the death of Iscariot. Nevertheless, I bid you get up and lead our troops against the Scot."

Now the hand of the Marquess veiled his countenance. But, "I am an ill man," he muttered, doggedly. "I cannot rise from this couch."

There was a silence.

"My lord," the Queen presently began, "without is an army prepared— ay, and quite able—to defend our England. The one requirement of this army is a leader. Afford them that, my lord—ah, I know that our peers are sold to the Bruce, yet our yeomen at least are honest. Give them, then, a leader, and they cannot but conquer, since God also is honest and incorruptible. Pardieu! a woman might lead these men, and lead them to victory!"

Hastings answered: "I am an ill man. I cannot rise from this couch."

You saw that Philippa was not beautiful. You perceived that to the contrary she was superb, saw the soul of the woman aglow, gilding the mediocrities of color and curve as a conflagration does a hovel.

"There is no man left in England," said the Queen, "since Sire Edward went into France. Praise God, I am his wife!" And she was gone without flurry.

Through the tent-flap Hastings beheld all that which followed. The English force was marshalled in four divisions, each commanded by a bishop and a baron. You could see the men fidgeting, puzzled by the delay; as a wind goes about a corn-field, vague rumors were going about those wavering spears. Toward them rode Philippa, upon a white palfrey, alone and perfectly tranquil. Her eight lieutenants were now gathered about her in voluble protestation, and she heard them out. Afterward she spoke, without any particular violence, as one might order a strange cur from his room. Then the Queen rode on, as though these eight declaiming persons had ceased to be of interest, and reined up before her standard-bearer, and took the standard in her hand. She began again to speak, and immediately the army was in an uproar; the barons were clustering behind her, in stealthy groups of two or three whisperers each; all were in the greatest amazement and knew not what to do; but the army was shouting the Queen's name.

"Now is England shamed," said Hastings, "since a woman alone dares to encounter the Scot. She will lead them into battle—and by God! there is no braver person under heaven than yonder Dutch Frau! Friend David, I perceive that your venture is lost, for those men would within the moment follow her to storm hell if she desired it."

He meditated and more lately shrugged. "And so would I," said Hastings.

A little afterward a gaunt and haggard old man, bare-headed and very hastily dressed, reined his horse by the Queen's side. "Madame and Queen," said Hastings, "I rejoice that my recent illness is departed. I shall, by God's grace, on this day drive the Bruce from England."

Philippa was not given to verbiage. Doubtless she had her emotions, but none was visible upon the honest face; yet one plump hand had fallen into the big-veined hand of Hastings. "I welcome back the gallant gentleman of yesterday. I was about to lead your army, my friend, since there was no one else to do it, but I was hideously afraid. At bottom every woman is a coward."

"You were afraid to do it," said the Marquess, "but you were going to do it, because there was no one else to do it! Ho, madame! had I an army of such cowards I would drive the Scot not past the Border but beyond the Orkneys."

The Queen then said, "But you are unarmed."

"Highness," he replied, "it is surely apparent that I, who have played the traitor to two monarchs within the same day, cannot with either decency or comfort survive that day." He turned upon the lords and bishops twittering about his horse's tail. "You merchandise, get back to your stations, and if there was ever an honest woman in any of your families, the which I doubt, contrive to get yourselves killed this day, as I mean to do, in the cause of the honestest and bravest woman our time has known." Immediately the English forces marched toward Merrington.

Philippa returned to her pavilion and inquired for John Copeland. He had ridden off, she was informed, armed, in company with five of her immediate retainers. She considered this strange, but made no comment.

You picture her, perhaps, as spending the morning in prayer, in beatings upon her breast, and in lamentations. Philippa did nothing of the sort. As you have heard, she considered her cause to be so clamantly just that to expatiate to the Holy Father upon its merits were an impertinence; it was not conceivable that He would fail her; and in any event, she had in hand a deal of sewing which required immediate attention. Accordingly she settled down to her needlework, while the Regent of England leaned his head against her knee, and his mother told him that ageless tale of Lord Huon, who in a wood near Babylon encountered the King of Faery, and subsequently stripped the atrocious Emir of both beard and daughter. All this the industrious woman narrated in a low and pleasant voice, while the wide-eyed Regent attended and at the proper intervals gulped his cough-mixture.

You must know that about noon Master John Copeland came into the tent. "We have conquered," he said. "Now, by the Face!"—thus, scoffingly, he used her husband's favorite oath—"now, by the Face! there was never a victory more complete! The Scottish army is as those sands which dried the letters King Ahasuerus gave the admirable Esther!"

"I rejoice," the Queen said, looking up from her sewing, "that we have conquered, though in nature I expected nothing else—Oh, horrible!" She sprang to her feet with a cry of anguish: and here in little you have the entire woman; the victory of her armament was to her a thing of course, since her cause was just, whereas the loss of two front teeth by John Copeland was a genuine calamity.

He drew her toward the tent-flap, which he opened. Without was a mounted knight, in full panoply, his arms bound behind him, surrounded by the Queen's five retainers. "In the rout I took him," said John Copeland; "though, as my mouth witnesses, I did not find this David Bruce a tractable prisoner."

"Is that, then, the King of Scots?" Philippa demanded, as she mixed salt and water for a mouth-wash; and presently: "Sire Edward should be pleased, I think. Will he not love me a little now, John Copeland?"

John Copeland lifted either plump hand toward his lips. "He could not choose," John Copeland said; "madame, he could no more choose but love you than I could choose."

Philippa sighed. Afterward she bade John Copeland rinse his gums and then take his prisoner to Hastings. He told her the Marquess was dead, slain by the Knight of Liddesdale. "That is a pity," the Queen said; and more lately: "There is left alive in England but one man to whom I dare entrust the keeping of the King of Scots. My barons are sold to him; if I retain Messire David by me, one or another lord will engineer his escape within the week, and Sire Edward will be vexed. Yet listen, John—" She unfolded her plan.

"I have long known," he said, when she had done, "that in all the world there was no lady more lovable. Twenty years I have loved you, my Queen, and yet it is but to-day I perceive that in all the world there is no lady more wise than you."

Philippa touched his cheek, maternally. "Foolish boy! You tell me the King of Scots has an arrow-wound in his nose? I think a bread poultice would be best.". . . So then John Copeland left the tent and presently rode away with his company.

Philippa saw that the Regent had his dinner, and afterward mounted her white palfrey and set out for the battle-field. There the Earl of Neville, as second in command, received her with great courtesy. God had shown to her Majesty's servants most singular favor despite the calculations of reasonable men—to which, she might remember, he had that morning taken the liberty to assent—some fifteen thousand Scots were slain. True, her gallant general was no longer extant, though this was scarcely astounding when one considered the fact that he had voluntarily entered the melee quite unarmed. A touch of age, perhaps; Hastings was always an eccentric man; and in any event, as epilogue, this Neville congratulated the Queen that—by blind luck, he was forced to concede—her worthy secretary had made a prisoner of the Scottish King. Doubtless, Master Copeland was an estimable scribe, and yet—Ah, yes, he quite followed her Majesty—beyond doubt, the wardage of a king was an honor not lightly to be conferred. Oh yes, he understood; her Majesty desired that the office should be given some person of rank. And pardie! her Majesty was in the right. Eh? said the Earl of Neville.

Intently gazing into the man's shallow eyes, Philippa assented. Master Copeland had acted unwarrantably in riding off with his captive. Let him be sought at once. She dictated a letter to Neville's secretary, which informed John Copeland that he had done what was not agreeable in purloining her prisoner without leave. Let him sans delay deliver the King to her good friend the Earl of Neville.

To Neville this was satisfactory, since he intended that once in his possession David Bruce should escape forthwith. The letter, I repeat, suited this smirking gentleman in its tiniest syllable, and the single difficulty was to convey it to John Copeland, for as to his whereabouts neither Neville nor any one else had the least notion.

JAMES BRANCH CABELL

This was immaterial, however, for they narrate that next day a letter signed with John Copeland's name was found pinned to the front of Neville's tent. I cite a passage therefrom: "I will not give up my royal prisoner to a woman or a child, but only to my own lord, Sire Edward, for to him I have sworn allegiance, and not to any woman. Yet you may tell the Queen she may depend on my taking excellent care of King David. I have poulticed his nose, as she directed."

Here was a nonplus, not perhaps without its comical side. Two great realms had met in battle, and the king of one of them had vanished like a soap-bubble. Philippa was in a rage—you could see that both by her demeanor and by the indignant letters she dictated; true, they could not be delivered, since they were all addressed to John Copeland. Meanwhile, Scotland was in despair, whereas the English barons were in a frenzy, because, however willing you may be, you cannot well betray your liege-lord to an unlocatable enemy. The circumstances were unique, and they remained unchanged for three feverish weeks.

We will now return to affairs in France, where on the day of the Nativity, as night gathered about Calais, John Copeland came unheralded to the quarters of King Edward, then besieging that city. Master Copeland entreated audience, and got it readily enough, since there was no man alive whom Sire Edward more cordially desired to lay his fingers upon.

A page brought Master Copeland to the King, a stupendous person, blond and incredibly big. With him were a careful Italian, that Almerigo di Pavia who afterward betrayed Sire Edward, and a lean soldier whom Master Copeland recognized as John Chandos. These three were drawing up an account of the recent victory at Cregi, to be forwarded to all mayors and sheriffs in England, with a cogent postscript as to the King's incidental and immediate need of money.

Now King Edward sat leaning far back in his chair, a hand on either hip, and his eyes narrowing as he regarded Master Copeland. Had the Brabanter flinched, the King would probably have hanged him within the next ten minutes; finding his gaze unwavering, the King was pleased. Here was a novelty; most people blinked quite genuinely under the scrutiny of those fierce big eyes, which were blue and cold and of an astounding lustre, gemlike as the March sea.

The King rose with a jerk and took John Copeland's hand. "Ha!" he grunted, "I welcome the squire who by his valor has captured the King of Scots. And now, my man, what have you done with Davie?"

John Copeland answered: "Highness, you may find him at your convenience safely locked in Bamborough Castle. Meanwhile, I entreat you, sire, do not take it amiss if I did not surrender King David to the orders of my lady Queen, for I hold my lands of you, and not of her, and my oath is to you, and not to her, unless indeed by choice."

"John," the King sternly replied, "the loyal service you have done us is considerable, whereas your excuse for kidnapping Davie is a farce. Hey, Almerigo, do you and Chandos avoid the chamber! I have something in private with this fellow." When they had gone, the King sat down and composedly said, "Now tell me the truth, John Copeland."

"Sire," he began, "it is necessary you first understand I bear a letter from Madame Philippa—"

"Then read it," said the King. "Heart of God! have I an eternity to waste on you Brabanters!"

John Copeland read aloud, while the King trifled with a pen, half negligent, and in part attendant.

Read John Copeland:

My Dear Lord,
    I recommend me to your lordship with soul and body and all my poor might, and with all this I thank you, as my dear lord, dearest and best beloved of all earthly lords I protest to me, and thank you, my dear lord, with all this as I say before. Your comfortable letter came to me on Saint Gregory's day, and I was never so glad as when I heard by your letter that ye were strong enough in Ponthieu by the grace of God for to keep you from your enemies. Among them I estimate Madame Catherine de Salisbury, who would have betrayed you to the Scot. And, dear lord, if it be pleasing to your high lordship that as soon as ye may that I might hear of your gracious speed, which may God Almighty continue and increase, I shall be glad, and also if ye do each night chafe your feet with a rag of woollen stuff. And, my dear lord, if it like you for to know of my fare, John Copeland will acquaint you concerning the Bruce his capture, and the syrup he brings for our son Lord Edward's cough, and the great malice-workers in these shires which would have so despitefully wrought to you, and of the manner of taking it after each meal. I am lately informed that Madame

Catherine is now at Stirling with Robert Stewart and has lost all her good looks through a fever. God is invariably gracious to His servants. Farewell, my dear lord, and may the Holy Trinity keep you from your adversaries and ever send me comfortable tidings of you. Written at York, in the Castle, on Saint Gregory's day last past, by your own poor

PHILIPPA.

To my true lord

"H'm!" said the King; "and now give me the entire story."

John Copeland obeyed. I must tell you that early in the narrative King Edward arose and, with a sob, strode toward a window. "Catherine!" he said. He remained motionless what time Master Copeland went on without any manifest emotion. When he had ended, King Edward said, "And where is Madame de Salisbury now?"

At this the Brabanter went mad. As a leopard springs he leaped upon the King, and grasping him by either shoulder, shook that monarch as one punishing a child.

"Now by the splendor of God—!" King Edward began, very terrible in his wrath. He saw that John Copeland held a dagger to his breast, and shrugged. "Well, my man, you perceive I am defenceless. Therefore make an end, you dog."

"First you will hear me out," John Copeland said.

"It would appear," the King retorted, "that I have little choice."

At this time John Copeland began: "Sire, you are the greatest monarch our race has known. England is yours, France is yours, conquered Scotland lies prostrate at your feet. To-day there is no other man in all the world who possesses a tithe of your glory; yet twenty years ago Madame Philippa first beheld you and loved you, an outcast, an exiled, empty-pocketed prince. Twenty years ago the love of Madame Philippa, great Count William's daughter, got for you the armament wherewith England was regained. Twenty years ago but for Madame Philippa you had died naked in some ditch."

"Go on," the King said presently.

"And afterward you took a fancy to reign in France. You learned then that we Brabanters are a frugal people: Madame Philippa was wealthy when she married you, and twenty years had but quadrupled her fortune. She gave you every penny of it that you might fit out this expedition; now her very crown is in pawn at Ghent. In fine, the love of

Madame Philippa gave you France as lightly as one might bestow a toy upon a child who whined for it."

The King fiercely said, "Go on."

"Eh, sire, I intend to. You left England undefended that you might posture a little in the eyes of Europe. And meanwhile a woman preserves England, a woman gives you all Scotland as a gift, and in return demands nothing—God ha' mercy on us!—save that you nightly chafe your feet with a bit of woollen. You hear of it—and ask, '*Where is Madame de Salisbury?*' Here beyond doubt is the cock of Æsop's fable," snarled John Copeland, "who unearthed a gem and grumbled that his diamond was not a grain of corn."

"You will be hanged ere dawn," the King replied, and yet by this one hand had screened his face. "Meanwhile spit out your venom."

"I say to you, then," John Copeland continued, "that to-day you are master of Europe. That but for this woman whom for twenty years you have neglected you would to-day be mouldering in some pauper's grave. Eh, without question, you most magnanimously loved that shrew of Salisbury! because you fancied the color of her eyes, Sire Edward, and admired the angle between her nose and her forehead. Minstrels unborn will sing of this great love of yours. Meantime I say to you"—now the man's rage was monstrous—"I say to you, go home to your too-tedious wife, the source of all your glory! sit at her feet! and let her teach you what love is!" He flung away the dagger. "There you have the truth. Now summon your attendants, my tres beau sire, and have me hanged."

The King gave no movement. "You have been bold—" he said at last.

"But you have been far bolder, sire. For twenty years you have dared to flout that love which is God made manifest as His main heritage to His children."

King Edward sat in meditation for a long while. "I consider my wife's clerk," he drily said, "to discourse of love in somewhat too much the tone of a lover." And a flush was his reward.

But when this Copeland spoke he was as one transfigured. His voice was grave and very tender.

"As the fish have their life in the waters, so I have and always shall have mine in love. Love made me choose and dare to emulate a lady, long ago, through whom I live contented, without expecting any other good. Her purity is so inestimable that I cannot say whether I derive more pride or sorrow from its pre-eminence. She does not love me, and she never will. She would condemn me to be hewed in fragments sooner than permit her husband's little finger to be injured. Yet she surpasses all others so utterly that I would rather hunger in her presence than enjoy from another all which a lover can devise."

Sire Edward stroked the table through this while, with an inverted pen. He cleared his throat. He said, half-fretfully:

"Now, by the Face! it is not given every man to love precisely in this troubadourish fashion. Even the most generous person cannot render to love any more than that person happens to possess. I had a vision once: The devil sat upon a cathedral spire and white doves flew about him. Monks came and told him to begone. 'Do not the spires show you, O son of darkness,' they clamored, 'that the place is holy?' And Satan (in my vision) said these spires were capable of various interpretations. I speak of symbols, John. Yet I also have loved, in my own fashion—and, it would seem, I win the same reward as you."

He said more lately: "And so she is at Stirling now? with Robert Stewart?" He laughed, not overpleasantly. "Eh, yes, it needed a bold person to bring all your tidings! But you Brabanters are a very thorough-going people."

The King rose and flung back his big head as a lion might. "John, the loyal service you have done us and our esteem for your valor are so great that they may well serve you as an excuse. May shame fall on those who bear you any ill-will! You will now return home, and take your prisoner, the King of Scotland, and deliver him to my wife, to do with as she may elect. You will convey to her my entreaty—not my orders, John— that she come to me here at Calais. As remuneration for this evening's insolence, I assign lands as near your house as you can choose them to the value of L500 a year for you and for your heirs."

You must know that John Copeland fell upon his knees before King Edward. "Sire—" he stammered.

But the King raised him. "Nay," he said, "you are the better man. Were there any equity in Fate, John Copeland, your lady had loved you, not me. As it is, I shall strive to prove not altogether unworthy of my fortune. Go, then, John Copeland—go, my squire, and bring me back my Queen."

Presently he heard John Copeland singing without. And through that instant was youth returned to Edward Plantagenet, and all the scents and shadows and faint sounds of Valenciennes on that ancient night when a tall girl came to him, running, stumbling in her haste to bring him kingship. Now at last he understood the heart of Philippa.

"Let me live!" the King prayed; "O Eternal Father, let me live a little while that I may make atonement!" And meantime John Copeland sang without and the Brabanter's heart was big with joy.

Sang John Copeland:

> *Long I besought thee, nor vainly,*
> *Daughter of water and air—*
> *Charis! Idalia! Hortensis!*
> *Hast thou not heard the prayer,*
> *When the blood stood still with loving,*
> *And the blood in me leapt like wine,*
> *And I murmured thy name, Melaenis?—*
> *That heard me, (the glory is thine!)*
> *And let the heart of Atys,*
> *At last, at last, be mine!*
>
> *Falsely they tell of thy dying,*
> *Thou that art older than Death,*
> *And never the Hoerselberg hid thee,*
> *Whatever the slanderer saith,*
> *For the stars are as heralds forerunning,*
> *When laughter and love combine*
> *At twilight, in thy light, Melaenis—*
> *That heard me, (the glory is thine!)*
> *And let the heart of Atys,*
> *At last, at last, be mine!*

THE END OF THE FIFTH NOVEL

VI

The Story of the Satraps

In the year of grace 1381 (Nicolas begins) was Dame Anne magnificently fetched from remote Bohemia, and at Westminster married to Sire Richard, the second monarch of that name to reign in England. The Queen had presently noted a certain priest who went forbiddingly about her court, where he was accorded a provisional courtesy, and more forbiddingly into many hovels, where day by day a pitiful wreckage of humanity both blessed and hoodwinked him, as he morosely knew, and adored him, as he never knew at all.

Queen Anne made inquiries. This young cleric was amanuensis to the Duke of Gloucester, she was informed, and notoriously a by-blow of the Duke's brother, the dead Lionel of Clarence. She sent for this Edward Maudelain. When he came her first perception was, "How wonderful his likeness to the King!" while the thought's commentary ran, unacknowledged, "Ay, as an eagle resembles a falcon!" For here, to the observant eye, was a more zealous person, already passion-wasted, and ineffably a more dictatorial and stiff-necked being than the lazy and amiable King; also, this Maudelain's face and nose were somewhat too long and high; and the priest was, in a word, the less comely of the pair by a very little, and by an infinity the more kinglike.

"You are my cousin now, messire," she told him, and innocently offered to his lips her own.

He never moved; but their glances crossed, and for that instant she saw the face of a man who has just stepped into a quicksand. She trembled, without knowing why. Then he spoke, composedly, and of trivial matters.

Thus began the Queen's acquaintance with Edward Maudelain. She was by this time the loneliest woman in the island. Her husband granted her a bright and fresh perfection of form and color, but desiderated any appetizing tang, and lamented, in his phrase, a certain kinship to the impeccable loveliness of some female saint in a jaunty tapestry; bright as ice in sunshine, just so her beauty chilled you, he complained: and moreover, this daughter of the Caesars had been fetched into England, chiefly, to breed him children, and this she had never done. Undoubtedly he had made a bad bargain—he was too easy-going, people presumed upon it. His barons snatched their cue and esteemed Dame Anne to be negligible; whereas the clergy, finding that she obstinately read the Scriptures in the vulgar tongue, under the irrelevant plea of not comprehending Latin, denounced her from their pulpits as a heretic and as the evil woman prophesied by Ezekiel.

It was the nature of this desolate child to crave affection, as a necessity almost, and pitifully she tried to purchase it through almsgiving. In the attempt she could have found no coadjutor more ready than Edward Maudelain. Giving was with these downright two a sort of obsession, though always he gave in a half scorn but half concealed; and presently they could have marshalled an army of adherents, all in rags, who would cheerfully have been hacked to pieces for either of the twain, and have praised God at the final gasp for the privilege. It was perhaps the tragedy of the man's life that he never suspected this.

Now in and about the Queen's unfrequented rooms the lonely woman and the priest met daily to discuss now this or that comminuted point of theology, or now (to cite a single instance) Gammer Tudway's obstinate sciatica. Considerate persons found something of the pathetic in their preoccupation by these trifles while, so clamantly, the dissension between the young King and his uncles gathered to a head: the air was thick with portents; and was this, then, an appropriate time, the judicious demanded of high Heaven, for the Queen of fearful England to concern herself about a peasant's toothache?

Long afterward was Edward Maudelain to remember this brief and tranquil period of his life, and to wonder over the man that he had been through this short while. Embittered and suspicious she had found him, noted for the carping tongue he lacked both power and inclination to bridle; and she had, against his nature, made Maudelain see that every person is at bottom lovable, and all vices but the stains of a traveller midway in a dusty journey; and had led the priest no longer to do good for his soul's health, but simply for his fellow's benefit.

And in place of that monstrous passion which had at first view of her possessed the priest, now, like a sheltered taper, glowed an adoration which yearned, in mockery of common-sense, to suffer somehow for this beautiful and gracious comrade; though very often a sudden pity for her loneliness and the knowledge that she dared trust no one save himself would throttle him like two assassins and move

JAMES BRANCH CABELL

the hot-blooded young man to an exquisite agony of self-contempt and exultation.

Now Maudelain made excellent songs, it was a matter of common report. Yet but once in their close friendship had the Queen commanded him to make a song for her. This had been at Dover, about vespers, in the starved and tiny garden overlooking the English Channel, upon which her apartments faced; and the priest had fingered his lute for an appreciable while before he sang, a thought more harshly than was his custom.

Sang Maudelain;

> *Ave Maria! now cry we so*
> *That see night wake and daylight go.*

> *Mother and Maid, in nothing incomplete,*
> *This night that gathers is more light and fleet*
> *Than twilight trod alway with stumbling feet,*
> *Agentes uno animo.*

> *Ever we touch the prize we dare not take!*
> *Ever we know that thirst we dare not slake!*
> *And ever to a dreamed-of goal we make—*
> *Est caeli in palatio!*

> *Yet long the road, and very frail are we*
> *That may not lightly curb mortality,*
> *Nor lightly tread together silently,*
> *Et carmen unum facio:*

> *Mater, ora filium,*
> *Ut post hoc exilium*
> *Nobis donet gaudium*
> *Beatorum omnium!*

Dame Anne had risen. She said nothing. She stayed in this posture for a lengthy while, reeling, one hand yet clasping either breast. More lately she laughed, and began to speak of Long Simon's recent fever. Was there no method of establishing him in another cottage? No, the priest said, the villiens, like the cattle, were by ordinary deeded with the land.

One day, about the hour of prime, in that season of the year when fields smell of young grass, the Duke of Gloucester sent for Edward Maudelain. The court was then at Windsor. The priest came quickly to his patron. He found the Duke in company with Edmund of York and bland Harry of Derby, John of Gaunt's oldest son. Each was a proud and handsome man. To-day Gloucester was gnawing at his finger nails, big York seemed half-asleep, and the Earl of Derby patiently to await something as yet ineffably remote.

"Sit down!" snarled Gloucester. His lean and evil countenance was that of a tired devil. The priest obeyed, wondering so high an honor should be accorded him in the view of three great noblemen. Then Gloucester said, in his sharp way: "Edward, you know, as England knows, the King's intention toward us three and our adherents. It has come to our demolishment or his. I confess a preference in the matter. I have consulted with the Pope concerning the advisability of taking the crown into my own hands. Edmund here does not want it, and John is already achieving one in Spain. Eh, in imagination I was already King of England, and I had dreamed—Well! to-day the prosaic courier arrived. Urban—the Neapolitan swine!—dares give me no assistance. It is decreed I shall never reign in these islands. And I had dreamed— Meanwhile, de Vere and de la Pole are at the King day and night, urging revolt. Within the week the three heads of us will embellish Temple Bar. You, of course, they will only hang."

"We must avoid England, then, my noble patron," the priest considered.

Angrily the Duke struck a clenched fist upon the table. "By the Cross! we remain in England, you and I and all of us. Others avoid. The Pope and the Emperor will have none of me. They plead for the Black Prince's heir, for the legitimate heir. Dompnedex! they shall have him!"

Maudelain recoiled, for he thought this twitching man insane.

"Besides, the King intends to take from me my fief at Sudbury," said the Duke of York, "in order he may give it to de Vere. That is both absurd and monstrous and abominable."

Openly Gloucester sneered. "Listen!" he rapped out toward Maudelain; "when they were drawing up the Great Peace at Bretigny, it happened, as is notorious, that the Black Prince, my brother, wooed in this town the Demoiselle Alixe Riczi, whom in the outcome he abducted. It is not as generally known, however, that, finding this

JAMES BRANCH CABELL

sister of the Vicomte do Montbrison a girl of obdurate virtue, he had prefaced the action by marriage."

"And what have I to do with all this?" said Edward Maudelain.

Gloucester retorted: "More than you think. For she was conveyed to Chertsey, here in England, where at the year's end she died in childbirth. A little before this time had Sir Thomas Holland seen his last day— the husband of that Joane of Kent whom throughout life my brother loved most marvellously. The disposition of the late Queen-Mother is tolerably well-known. I make no comment save that to her moulding my brother was as so much wax. In fine, the two lovers were presently married, and their son reigns to-day in England. The abandoned son of Alixe Riczi was reared by the Cistercians at Chertsey, where some years ago I found you—sire."

He spoke with a stifled voice, and wrenching forth each sentence; and now with a stiff forefinger flipped a paper across the table. "*In extremis* my brother did far more than confess. He signed—your Grace," said Gloucester. The Duke on a sudden flung out his hands, like a wizard whose necromancy fails, and the palms were bloodied where his nails had cut the flesh.

"Moreover, my daughter was born at Sudbury," said the Duke of York.

And of Maudelain's face I cannot tell you. He made pretence to read the paper carefully, but ever his eyes roved, and he knew that he stood among wolves. The room was oddly shaped, with eight equal sides; the ceiling was of a light and brilliant blue, powdered with many golden stars, and the walls were hung with smart tapestries which commemorated the exploits of Theseus. "King," this Maudelain said aloud, "of France and England, and Lord of Ireland, and Duke of Aquitaine! I perceive that Heaven loves a jest." He wheeled upon Gloucester and spoke with singular irrelevance: "And the titular Queen?"

Again the Duke shrugged. "I had not thought of the dumb wench. We have many convents."

And now Maudelain twisted the paper between his long, wet fingers and appeared to meditate.

"It would be advisable, your Grace," observed the Earl of Derby, suavely, and breaking his silence for the first time, "that yourself should wed Dame Anne, once the Apostolic See has granted the necessary dispensation. Treading too close upon the impendent death of our nominal lord the so-called King, the foreign war perhaps necessitated by her exile would be highly inconvenient."

Then these three princes rose and knelt before the priest; in long bright garments they were clad, and they glittered with gold and many jewels, what while he standing among them shuddered in his sombre robe. "Hail, King of England!" cried these three.

"Hail, ye that are my kinsmen!" he answered; "hail, ye that spring of an accursed race, as I! And woe to England for that fearful hour wherein Foulques the Querulous held traffic with a devil and on her begot the first of us Plantagenets! Of ice and of lust and of hell-fire are all we sprung; old records attest it; and fickle and cold and ravenous and without shame are we Plantagenets until the end. Of your brother's dishonor ye make merchandise to-day, and to-day fratricide whispers me, and leers, and, Heaven help me! I attend. O God of Gods! wilt Thou dare bid a man live stainless, having aforetime filled his veins with such a venom? Then haro, will I cry from Thy deepest hell. . . Nay, now let Lucifer rejoice for that his descendants know of what wood to make a crutch! You are very wise, my kinsmen. Take your measures, messieurs who are my kinsmen! Though were I any other than a Plantagenet, with what expedition would I now kill you that recognize the strength to do it! then would I slay you! without any animosity, would I slay you then, and just as I would kill as many splendid snakes!"

He went away, laughing horribly. Gloucester drummed upon the table, his brows contracted. But the lean Duke said nothing; big York seemed to drowse; and Henry of Derby smiled as he sounded a gong for that scribe who would draw up the necessary letters. The Earl's time was not yet come, but it was nearing.

In the antechamber the priest encountered two men-at-arms dragging a dead body from the castle. The Duke of Kent, Maudelain was informed, had taken a fancy to a peasant girl, and in remonstrance her misguided father had actually tugged at his Grace's sleeve.

Maudelain went first into the park of Windsor, where he walked for a long while alone. It was a fine day in the middle spring; and now he seemed to understand for the first time how fair his England was. For entire England was his splendid fief, held in vassalage to God and to no man alive, his heart now sang; allwhither his empire spread, opulent in grain and metal and every revenue of the earth, and in stalwart men (his chattels), and in strong orderly cities, where the windows would be adorned with scarlet hangings, and women (with golden hair and red lax lips) would presently admire as King Edward rode slowly by at the head of a resplendent retinue. And always the King would bow,

JAMES BRANCH CABELL

graciously and without haste, to his shouting people. . . He laughed to find himself already at rehearsal of the gesture.

It was strange, though, that in this glorious fief of his so many persons should, as yet, live day by day as cattle live, suspicious of all other moving things (with reason), and roused from their incurious and filthy apathy only when some glittering baron, like a resistless eagle, swept uncomfortably near on some by-errand of the more bright and windy upper-world. East and north they had gone yearly, for so many centuries, these dumb peasants, like herded sheep, so that in the outcome their carcasses might manure the soil of France yonder or of more barren Scotland. Give these serfs a king, now, who (being absolute), might dare to deal in perfect equity with rich and poor, who with his advent would bring Peace into England as his bride, as Trygaeus did very anciently in Athens—"And then," the priest paraphrased, "may England recover all the blessings she has lost, and everywhere the glitter of active steel will cease." For everywhere men would crack a rustic jest or two, unhurriedly. The vivid fields would blacken under their sluggish ploughs, and they would find that with practice it was almost as easy to chuckle as it was to cringe.

Meanwhile on every side the nobles tyrannized in their degree, well clothed and nourished, but at bottom equally comfortless in condition. As illuminate by lightning Maudelain saw the many factions of his barons squabbling for gross pleasures, like wolves over a corpse, and blindly dealing death to one another to secure at least one more delicious gulp before that inevitable mangling by the teeth of some burlier colleague. The complete misery of England showed before him like a winter landscape. The thing was questionless. He must tread henceforward without fear among frenzied beasts, and to their ultimate welfare. On a sudden Maudelain knew himself to be strong and admirable throughout, and hesitancy ebbed.

True, Richard, poor fool, must die. Squarely the priest faced that stark and hideous circumstance; to spare Richard was beyond his power, and the boy was his brother; yes, this oncoming king would be in effect a fratricide, and after death irrevocably damned. To burn, and eternally to burn, and, worst of all, to know that the torment was eternal! ay, it would be hard; but, at the cost of one ignoble life and one inconsiderable soul, to win so many men to manhood bedazzled his every faculty, in anticipation of the exploit.

The tale tells that Maudelain went toward the little garden he knew so well which adjoined Dame Anne's apartments. He found the Queen there, alone, as nowadays she was for the most part, and he paused to wonder at her bright and singular beauty. How vaguely odd it was, he reflected, too, how alien in its effect to that of any other woman in sturdy England, and how associable it was, somehow, with every wild and gracious denizen of the woods which blossomed yonder.

In this place the world was all sunlight, temperate but undiluted. They had met in a wide, unshaded plot of grass, too short to ripple, which everywhere glowed steadily, like a gem. Right and left birds sang as in a contest. The sky was cloudless, a faint and radiant blue throughout, save where the sun stayed as yet in the zenith, so that the Queen's brows cast honey-colored shadows upon either cheek. The priest was greatly troubled by the proud and heatless brilliancies, the shrill joys, of every object within the radius of his senses.

She was splendidly clothed, in a kirtle of very bright green, tinted like the verdancy of young ferns in sunlight, and over all a gown of white, cut open on either side as far as the hips. This garment was embroidered with golden leopards and trimmed with ermine. About her yellow hair was a chaplet of gold, wherein emeralds glowed. Her blue eyes were as large and bright and changeable (he thought) as two oceans in midsummer; and Maudelain stood motionless and seemed to himself but to revere, as the Earl Ixion did, some bright and never stable wisp of cloud, while somehow all elation departed from him as water does from a wetted sponge compressed. He laughed discordantly; but within the moment his sun-lit face was still and glorious, like that of an image.

"Wait—! O my only friend—!" said Maudelain. Then in a level voice he told her all, unhurriedly and without any sensible emotion.

She had breathed once, with an aweful inhalation. She had screened her countenance from his gaze what while you might have counted fifty. More lately the lithe body of Dame Anne was alert, as one suddenly aroused from dreaming. "This means more war, for de Vere and Tressilian and de la Pole and Bramber and others of the barons know that the King's fall signifies their ruin. Many thousands die to-morrow."

He answered, "It means a brief and cruel war."

"In that war the nobles will ride abroad with banners and gay surcoats, and kill and ravish in the pauses of their songs; while daily in that war the naked peasants will kill the one the other, without knowing why."

His thought had forerun hers. "Many would die, but in the end I would be King, and the general happiness would rest at my disposal.

The adventure of this world is wonderful, and it goes otherwise than under the strict tutelage of reason."

"Not yours, but Gloucester's and his barons'. Friend, they would set you on the throne to be their puppet and to move only as they pulled the strings. Thwart them and they will fling you aside, as the barons have dealt aforetime with every king that dared oppose them. Nay, they desire to live pleasantly, to have fish o' Fridays, and white bread and the finest wine the whole year through, and there is not enough for all, say they. Can you alone contend against them? and conquer them? then only do I bid you reign."

The sun had grown too bright, too merciless, but as always she drew the truth from him, even to his agony. "I cannot. I would not endure a fortnight. Heaven help us, nor you nor I nor any one may transform of any personal force this bitter time, this piercing, cruel day of frost and sun. Charity and Truth are excommunicate, and the King is only an adorned and fearful person who leads wolves toward their quarry, lest, lacking it, they turn and devour him. Everywhere the powerful labor to put one another out of worship, and each to stand the higher with the other's corpse as his pedestal; and always Lechery and Hatred sway these proud and inconsiderate fools as winds blow at will the gay leaves of autumn. We but fight with gaudy shadows, we but aspire to overpass a mountain of unstable sand! We two alone of all the scuffling world! Oh, it is horrible, and I think that Satan plans the jest! We dream a while of refashioning this bleak universe, and we know that we alone can do it! and we are as demigods, you and I, in those gallant dreams! and at the end we can but poultice some dirty rascal!"

The Queen answered sadly: "Once did God tread the tangible world, for a very little while, and, look you, to what trivial matters He devoted that brief space! Only to chat with fishermen, and to reason with lost women, and habitually to consort with rascals, till at last He might die between two cutpurses, ignominiously! Were the considerate persons of His day moved at all by the death of this fanatic? I bid you now enumerate through what long halls did the sleek heralds proclaim His crucifixion! and the armament of great-jowled emperors that were distraught by it?"

He answered: "It is true. Of anise even and of cumin the Master estimates His tithe—" Maudelain broke off with a yapping laugh. "Puf! He is wiser than we. I am King of England. It is my heritage."

"It means war. Many will die, many thousands will die, and to no betterment of affairs."

"I am King of England. I am Heaven's satrap here, and answerable to Heaven alone. It is my heritage." And now his large and cruel eyes flamed as he regarded her.

And visibly beneath their glare the woman changed. "My friend, must I not love you any longer? You would be content with happiness? I am jealous of that happiness! for you are the one friend that I have had, and so dear to me—Look you!" she said, with a light, wistful laugh, "there have been times when I was afraid of everything you touched, and I hated everything you looked at. I would not have you stained; I desired but to pass my whole life between the four walls of some dingy and eternal gaol, forever alone with you, lest you become as other men. I would in that period have been the very bread you eat, the least perfume which delights you, the clod you touch in crushing it, and often I have loathed some pleasure I derived from life because I might not transfer it to you undiminished. For I wanted somehow to make you happy to my own anguish. . . It was wicked, I suppose, for the imagining of it made me happy, too."

Throughout she spoke as simply as a child.

And beside him Maudelain's hands had fallen like so much lead, and remembering his own nature, he longed for annihilation only, before she had appraised his vileness. In consequence he said:

"With reason Augustine crieth out against the lust of the eyes. 'For pleasure seeketh objects beautiful, melodious, fragrant, savory, and soft; but this disease those contrary as well, not for the sake of suffering annoyance, but out of the lust of making trial of them!' Ah! ah! too curiously I planned my own damnation, too presumptuously I had esteemed my soul a worthy scapegoat, and I had gilded my enormity with many lies. Yet indeed, indeed, I had believed brave things, I had planned a not ignoble bargain—! Ey, say, is it not laughable, madame?— as my birthright Heaven accords me a penny, and with that only penny I must anon be seeking to bribe Heaven."

Presently he said: "Yet are we indeed God's satraps, as but now I cried in my vainglory, and we hold within our palms the destiny of many peoples. Depardieux! He is wiser than we are, it may be! And as always Satan offers no unhandsome bribes—bribes that are tangible and sure."

They stood like effigies, lit by the broad, unsparing splendor of the morning, but again their kindling eyes had met, and again the man shuddered visibly, convulsed by a monstrous and repulsive joy. "Decide!

JAMES BRANCH CABELL

oh, decide very quickly, my only friend!" he wailed, "for throughout I am all filth!"

Closer she drew to him and without hesitancy laid one hand on either shoulder. "O my only friend!" she breathed, with red lax lips which were very near to his, "throughout so many years I have ranked your friendship as the chief of all my honors! and I pray God with an entire heart that I may die so soon as I have done what I must do to-day!"

Almost did Edward Maudelain smile, but now his stiffening mouth could not complete the brave attempt. "God save King Richard!" said the priest. "For by the cowardice and greed and ignorance of little men were Salomon himself confounded, and by them is Hercules lightly unhorsed. Were I Leviathan, whose bones were long ago picked clean by pismires, I could perform nothing. Therefore do you pronounce my doom."

"O King," then said Dame Anne, "I bid you go forever from the court and live forever a landless man, and friendless, and without even name. I bid you dare to cast aside all happiness and wealth and comfort and each common tie that even a pickpocket may boast, like tawdry and unworthy garments. In fine, I bid you dare be King and absolute, yet not of England—but of your own being, alike in motion and in thought and even in wish. This doom I dare adjudge and to pronounce, since we are royal and God's satraps, you and I."

Twice or thrice his dry lips moved before he spoke. He was aware of innumerable birds that carolled with a piercing and intolerable sweetness. "O Queen!" he hoarsely said, "O fellow satrap! Heaven has many fiefs. A fair province is wasted and accords no revenue. Therein waste beauty and a shrewd wit and an illimitable charity which of their pride go in fetters and achieve no increase. To-day the young King junkets with his flatterers, and but rarely thinks of England. You have that beauty in desire of which many and many a man would blithely enter hell, and the mere sight of which may well cause a man's voice to tremble as my voice trembles now, and in desire of which—But I tread afield! Of that beauty you have made no profit. O daughter of the Caesars, I bid you now gird either loin for an unlovely traffic. Old Legion must be fought with fire. True that the age is sick, that we may not cure, we can but salve the hurt—" Now had his hand torn open his sombre gown, and the man's bared breast shone in the sunlight, and everywhere heaved on it sleek and glittering beads of sweat. Twice he cried the Queen's name aloud, without prefix. In a while he said: "I bid you weave incessantly such snares of brain and body as may lure King Richard to be swayed by you, until against his will you daily guide this shallow-hearted fool to some commendable action. I bid you live as other folk do hereabouts. Coax! beg! cheat! wheedle! lie!" he barked like a teased dog, "till you achieve in part the task which is denied me. This doom I dare adjudge and to pronounce, since we are royal and God's satraps, you and I."

She answered with a tiny, wordless sound. He prayed for even horror as he appraised his handiwork. But presently, "I take my doom," the Queen proudly said. "I shall be lonely now, my only friend, and yet—it does not matter," the Queen said, with a little shiver. "No, nothing will ever greatly matter now, I think."

Her eyes had filled with tears; she was unhappy, and as always this knowledge roused in Maudelain a sort of frenzied pity and a hatred, quite illogical, of all other things existent. She was unhappy, that only he realized; and half way he had strained a soft and groping hand toward his lips when he relinquished it. "Nay, not even that," said Edward Maudelain, very proudly, too, and now at last he smiled; "since we are God's satraps, you and I."

Afterward he stood thus for an appreciable silence, with ravenous eyes, motionless save that behind his back his fingers were bruising one another. Everywhere was this or that bright color and an incessant melody. It was unbearable. Then it was over; the ordered progress of all happenings was apparent, simple, and natural; and contentment came into his heart like a flight of linnets over level fields at dawn. He left her, and as he went he sang.

Sang Maudelain:

> *Christ save us all, as well He can,*
> *A solis ortus cardine!*
> *For He is both God and man,*
> *Qui natus est de virgine,*
> *And we but part of His wide plan*
> *That sing, and heartily sing we,*
> *"Gloria Tibi, Domine!"*
>
> *Between a heifer and an ass*
> *Enixa est puerpera;*

JAMES BRANCH CABELL

In ragged woollen clad He was
Qui regnat super aethera,
And patiently may we then pass
That sing, and heartily sing we,
'Gloria Tibi, Domine!

The Queen shivered in the glad sunlight. "I am, it must be, pitiably weak," she said at last, "because I cannot sing as he does. And, since I am not very wise, were he to return even now—But he will not return. He will never return," the Queen repeated, carefully, and over and over again. "It is strange I cannot comprehend that he will never return! Ah, Mother of God!" she cried, with a steadier voice, "grant that I may weep! nay, of thy infinite mercy let me presently find the heart to weep!" And about the Queen of England many birds sang joyously.

Next day the English barons held a council, and in the midst of it King Richard demanded to be told his age.

"Your Grace is in your twenty-second year," said the uneasy Gloucester, and now with reason troubled, since he had been seeking all night long for the evanished Maudelain.

"Then I have been under tutors and governors longer than any other ward in my dominion. My lords, I thank you for your past services, but I need them no more." They had no check handy, and Gloucester in particular foreread his death-warrant, but of necessity he shouted with the others, "Hail, King of England!"

That afternoon the King's assumption of all royal responsibility was commemorated by a tournament, over which Dame Anne presided. Sixty of her ladies led as many knights by silver chains into the tilting-grounds at Smithfield, and it was remarked that the Queen appeared unusually mirthful. The King was in high good humor, already a pattern of conjugal devotion; and the royal pair retired at dusk to the Bishop of London's palace at Saint Paul's, where was held a merry banquet, with dancing both before and after supper.

THE END OF THE SIXTH NOVEL

VII

The Story of the Heritage

I n the year of grace 1399 (Nicolas begins) dwelt in a hut near Caer Dathyl in Arvon, as he had done for some five years, a gaunt hermit, notoriously consecrate, whom neighboring Welshmen revered as the Blessed Evrawc. There had been a time when people called him Edward Maudelain, but this period he dared not often remember.

For though in macerations of the flesh, in fasting, and in hour-long prayers he spent his days, this holy man was much troubled by devils. He got little rest because of them. Sometimes would come into his hut Belphegor in the likeness of a butler, and whisper, "Sire, had you been King, as was your right, you had drunk to-day not water but the wines of Spain and Hungary." Or Asmodeus saying, "Sire, had you been King, as was your right, you had lain now on cushions of silk."

One day in early spring came a more cunning devil, named Bembo, in the likeness of a fair woman with yellow hair and large blue eyes. She wore a massive crown which seemed too heavy for her frailness to sustain. Soft tranquil eyes had lifted from her book. "You are my cousin now, messire," this phantom had appeared to say.

That was the worst, and Maudelain began to fear he was a little mad because even this he had resisted with many aves.

There came also to his hut, through a sullen snowstorm, upon the afternoon of All Soul's day, a horseman in a long cloak of black. He tethered his black horse without and strode softly through the door, and upon his breast and shoulders the snow was white as the bleached bones of those women that died in Merlin's youth.

"Greetings in God's name, Messire Edward Maudelain," the stranger said.

Since the new-comer spoke intrepidly of holy things a cheerier Maudelain knew that this at least was no demon. "Greetings!" he answered. "But I am Evrawc. You name a man long dead."

"But it is from a certain Bohemian woman I come. What matter, then, if the dead receive me?" And thus speaking, the stranger dropped his cloak.

In flame-colored satin he was clad, which shimmered with each movement like a high flame, and his countenance had throughout the color and the glow of amber. His eyes were dark and very tender, and the tears somehow had come to Maudelain's eyes because of a sudden and great love for this tall stranger. "Eh, from the dead to the dead I travel, as ever, with a message and a token. My message runs, *Time is, O fellow satrap!* and my token is this."

And in this packet, wrapped with white parchment and tied with a golden cord, was only a lock of hair. It lay like a little yellow serpent in Maudelain's palm. "And yet five years ago," he mused, "this hair was turned to dust. God keep us all!" Then he saw the tall lean emissary puffed out like a candle-flame; and upon the floor he saw the huddled cloak waver and spread like ink, and the white parchment slowly dwindle, as snow melts under the open sun. But in his hand remained the lock of yellow hair.

"O my only friend," said Maudelain, "I may not comprehend, but I know that by no unhallowed art have you won back to me." Hair by hair he scattered what he held upon the floor. "*Time is!* and I have not need of any token wherewith to spur my memory." He prized up a corner of the hearthstone, took out a small leather bag, and that day purchased a horse and a sword.

At dawn the Blessed Evrawc rode eastward in this novel guise. It was two weeks later when he came to Sunninghill; and it happened that the same morning the Earl of Salisbury, who had excellent reason to consider. . .

Follows a lacuna of fourteen pages. Maudelain's successful imposture of Richard the Second, so strangely favored by their physical resemblance, and the subsequent fiasco at Circencester, are now, however, tolerably notorious. It would seem evident, from the Argument of the story in hand, that Nicolas attributes a large part of this mysterious business to the co-operancy of Isabel of Valois, King Richard's infant wife. And (should one have a taste for the deductive) the foregoing mention of Bembo, when compared with "THE STORY OF THE SCABBARD," would certainly hint that Owain Glyndwyr had a finger in the affair.

It is impossible to divine by what method, according to Nicolas, this Edward Maudelain was eventually substituted for his younger brother. Nicolas, if you are to believe his "EPILOGUE," had the best of reasons for knowing that the prisoner locked up in Pontefract Castle

. . . and eight men-at-arms followed him.

Quickly Maudelain rose from the table, pushing his tall chair aside, and in the act one fellow closed the door securely. "Nay, eat your fill, Sire Richard," said Piers Exton, "since you will not ever eat again."

"Is it so?" the trapped man answered quietly. "Then indeed you come in a good hour." Once only he smote upon his breast. "*Mea culpa!* O Eternal Father, do Thou shrive me very quickly of all those sins I have committed, both in thought and deed, for now the time is very short."

And Exton spat upon the dusty floor. "Foh, they had told me I would find a king here. I discover only a cat that whines."

"Then 'ware his claws!" As a viper leaps Maudelain sprang upon the nearest fellow and wrested away his halberd. "Then 'ware his claws, my men! For I come of an accursed race. And now let some of you lament that fearful hour wherein Foulques the Querulous held traffic with a demon and on her begot the first of us Plantagenets! For of ice and of lust and of hell-fire are all we sprung; old records attest it; and fickle and cold and ravenous and without fear are all we Plantagenets until the end. Ay, until the end! O God of Gods!" this Maudelain cried, with a great voice, "wilt Thou dare bid a man die patiently, having aforetime filled his veins with such a venom! Nay, I lack the grace to die as all Thy saints, without one carnal blow struck in my own defence. I lack the grace, my Father, for even at the last the devil's blood You gave me is not quelled. I dare atone for that old sin done by my father in the flesh, but yet I must atone as a Plantagenet!"

Then it was he and not they who pressed to the attack. Their meeting was a bloody business, for in that dark and crowded room Maudelain raged among his nine antagonists as an angered lion among wolves.

They struck at random and cursed shrilly, for they were now half-afraid of this prey they had entrapped; so that presently he was all hacked and bleeding, though as yet he had no mortal wound. Four of these men he had killed by this, and Piers Exton also lay at his feet.

Then the other four drew back a little. "Are ye tired so soon?" said Maudelain, and he laughed terribly. "What, even you! Why, look ye, my bold veterans, I never killed before to-day, and I am not breathed as yet."

Thus he boasted, exultant in his strength. But the other men saw that behind him Piers Exton had crawled into the chair from which (they thought) King Richard had just risen, and stood erect upon the cushions of it. They saw this Exton strike the King with his pole-axe, from behind, and once only, and they knew no more was needed.

"By God!" said one of them in the ensuing stillness, and it was he who bled the most, "that was a felon's blow."

But the dying man who lay before them made as though to smile. "I charge you all to witness," he faintly said, "how willingly I render to Caesar's daughter that which was ever hers."

Then Exton fretted, as with a little trace of shame: "Who would have thought the rascal had remembered that first wife of his so long? Caesar's daughter, saith he! and dares *in extremis* to pervert Holy Scripture like any Wycliffite! Well, he is as dead as that first Caesar now, and our gracious King, I think, will sleep the better for it. And yet—God only knows! for they are an odd race, even as he said—these Plantagenets."

THE END OF THE SEVENTH NOVEL

VIII

The Story of the Scabbard

In the year of grace 1400 (Nicolas begins) King Richard, the second monarch of that name to rule in England, wrenched his own existence, and nothing more, from the close wiles of Bolingbroke. The circumstances have been recorded otherwhere. All persons, saving only Owain Glyndwyr and Henry of Lancaster, believed King Richard dead at that period when Richard attended his own funeral, as a proceeding taking to the fancy, and, among many others, saw the body of Edward Maudelain interred with every regal ceremony in the chapel at Langley Bower. Then alone Sire Richard crossed the seas, and at thirty-three set out to inspect a transformed and gratefully untrammelling world wherein not a foot of land belonged to him.

Holland was the surname he assumed, the name of his half-brothers; and to detail his Asian wanderings were both tedious and unprofitable. But at the end of each four months would come to him a certain messenger from Glyndwyr, whom Richard supposed to be the devil Bembo, who notoriously ran every day around the world upon the Welshman's business. It was in the Isle of Taprobane, where the pismires are as great as hounds, and mine and store the gold the inhabitants afterward rob them of through a very cunning device, that this emissary brought the letter which read simply, "Now is England fit pasture for the White Hart." Presently was Richard Holland in Wales, and then he rode to Sycharth.

There, after salutation, Glyndwyr gave an account of his long stewardship. It was a puzzling record of obscure and tireless machinations with which we have no immediate concern: in brief, the very barons who had ousted King Log had been the first to find King Stork intolerable; and Northumberland, Worcester, Douglas, Mortimer, and so on, were already pledged and in open revolt. "By the God I do not altogether serve," Owain ended, "you have but to declare yourself, sire, and within the moment England is yours."

More lately Richard spoke with narrowed eyes. "You forget that while Henry of Lancaster lives no other man will ever reign out a tranquil week in these islands. Come then! the hour strikes; and we will coax the devil for once in a way to serve God."

"Oh, but there is a boundary appointed," Glyndwyr moodily returned. "You, too, forget that in cold blood this Henry stabbed my best-loved son. But I do not forget this, and I have tried divers methods which we need not speak of—I who can at will corrupt the air, and cause sickness and storms, raise heavy mists, and create plagues and fires and shipwrecks; yet the life itself I cannot take. For there is a boundary appointed, sire, and in the end the Master of our Sabbaths cannot serve us even though he would."

And Richard crossed himself. "You horribly mistake my meaning. Your practices are your own affair, and in them I decline to dabble. I design but to trap a tiger with his appropriate bait. For you have a fief at Caer Idion, I think?—Very well! I intend to herd your sheep there, for a week or two, after the honorable example of Apollo. It is your part merely to see that Henry knows I live alone and in disguise at Caer Idion."

The gaunt Welshman chuckled. "Yes, Bolingbroke would cross the world, much less the Severn, to make quite sure of Richard's death. He would come in his own person with at most some twenty followers. I will have a hundred there; and certain aging scores will then be settled in that place." Glyndwyr meditated afterward, very evilly. "Sire," he said without prelude, "I do not recognize Richard of Bordeaux. You have garnered much in travelling!"

"Why, look you," Richard returned, "I have garnered so much that I do not greatly care whether this scheme succeed or no. With age I begin to contend even more indomitably that a wise man will consider nothing very seriously. You barons here believe it an affair of importance who may chance to be the King of England, say, this time next year; you take sides between Henry and myself. I tell you frankly that neither of us, that no man in the world, by reason of innate limitations, can ever rule otherwise than abominably, or, ruling, create anything save discord. Nor can I see how this matters either, since the discomfort of an ant-village is not, after all, a planet-wrecking disaster. Nay, if the planets do indeed sing together, it is, depend upon it, to the burden of *Fools All*. For I am as liberally endowed as most people; and when I consider my abilities, performances, instincts, and so on, quite aloofly, as I would those of another person, I can only shrug: and to conceive that common-sense, much less Omnipotence, would ever concern itself about the actions of a creature so entirely futile is, to me at least, impossible."

"I have known the thought," said Owain—"though rarely since I found the Englishwoman that was afterward my wife, and never since my son, my Grunyd, was murdered by a jesting man. He was more like me than the others, people said. . . You are as yet the empty scabbard, powerless alike for help or hurt. Ey, hate or love must be the sword, sire, that informs us here, and then, if only for a little while, we are as gods."

"Pardie! I have loved as often as Salomon, and in fourteen kingdoms."

"We of Cymry have a saying, sire, that when a man loves par amours the second time he may safely assume that he has never been in love at all."

"And I hate Henry of Lancaster as I do the devil."

"I greatly fear," said Owain with a sigh, "lest it may be your irreparable malady to hate nothing, not even that which you dislike."

So then Glyndwyr rode south to besiege and burn the town of Caerdyf, while at Caer Idion Richard Holland tranquilly abode for some three weeks. There was in this place only Caradawc (the former shepherd), his wife Alundyne, and their sole daughter Branwen. They gladly perceived Sire Richard was no more a peasant than he was a curmudgeon; as Caradawc observed: "It is perfectly apparent that the robe of Padarn Beisrudd would fit him as a glove does the hand, but we will ask no questions, since it is not wholesome to dispute the orderings of Owain Glyndwyr."

They did not; and later day by day would Richard Holland drive the flocks to pasture near the Severn, and loll there in the shade, and make songs to his lute. He grew to love this leisured life of bright and open spaces; and its long solitudes, grateful with the warm odors of growing things and with poignant bird-noises, and the tranquillity of these meadows, that were always void of hurry, bedrugged the man through many fruitless and incurious hours.

Each day at noon would Branwen bring his dinner, and sometimes chat with him while he ate. After supper he would discourse to Branwen of remote kingdoms, wherethrough he had ridden at adventure, as the wind veers, among sedate and alien peoples who adjudged him a madman; and she, in turn, would tell him many curious tales from the *Red Book of Hergest*—as of Gwalchmai, and Peredur, and Geraint, in each one of whom she had presently discerned an inadequate forerunnership of Richard's existence.

This Branwen was a fair wench, slender as a wand, and, in a harmless way, of a bold demeanor twin to that of a child who is ignorant of evil and in consequence of suspicion. Happily, though, had she been named for that unhappy lady of old, the wife of King Matholwch, for this Branwen, too, had a white, thin, wistful face, like that of an empress on a silver coin which is a little worn. Her eyes were large and brilliant, colored like clear emeralds, and her abundant hair was so much cornfloss, only more brightly yellow and of immeasurably finer texture. In full sunlight her cheeks were frosted like the surface of a peach, but the underlying cool pink of them was rather that of a cloud, Richard decided. In all, a taking morsel! though her shapely hands were hard with labor, and she rarely laughed; for, as in recompense, her heart was tender and ignorant of discontent, and she rarely ceased to smile as over some peculiar and wonderful secret which she intended, in due time, to share with you alone. Branwen had many lovers, and preferred among them young Gwyllem ap Llyr, a portly lad, who was handsome enough, for all his tiny and piggish eyes, and sang divinely.

Presently this Gwyllem came to Richard with two quarter-staves. "Saxon," he said, "you appear a stout man. Take your pick of these, then, and have at you."

"Such are not the weapons I would have named," Richard answered, "yet in reason, messire, I may not deny you."

With that they laid aside their coats and fell to exercise. In these unaccustomed bouts Richard was soundly drubbed, as he had anticipated, but throughout he found himself the stronger man, and he managed somehow to avoid an absolute overthrow. By what method he never ascertained.

"I have forgotten what we are fighting about," he observed, after a half-hour of this; "or, to be perfectly exact, I never knew. But we will fight no more in this place. Come and go with me to Welshpool, Messire Gwyllem, and there we will fight to a conclusion over good sack and claret."

"Content!" cried Gwyllem; "but only if you yield me Branwen."

"Have we indeed wasted a whole half-hour in squabbling over a woman?" Richard demanded; "like two children in a worldwide toyshop over any one particular toy? Then devil take me if I am not heartily ashamed of my folly! Though, look you, Gwyllem, I would speak naught save commendation of these delicate and livelily-tinted creatures so long as one is able to approach them in a proper spirit of levity: it is only their not infrequent misuse which I would condemn; and in my opinion the person who elects to build a shrine for any one of them has only himself to blame if his divinity will ascend no pedestal save the carcass of his happiness. Yet have many men since time was young been addicted to the practice, as were Hercules and Merlin to their illimitable sorrow; and, indeed, the more I reconsider the old gallantries of Salomon, and of other venerable and sagacious potentates, the more profoundly am I ashamed of my sex."

Gwyllem said: "That is all very fine. Perhaps it is also reasonable. Only when you love you do not reason."

"I was endeavoring to prove that," said Richard gently. Then they went to Welshpool, ride and tie on Gwyllem's horse. Tongue loosened by the claret, Gwyllem raved aloud of Branwen, like a babbling faun, while to each rapture Richard affably assented. In his heart he likened the boy to Dionysos at Naxos, and could find no blame for Ariadne. Moreover, the room was comfortably dark and cool, for thick vines hung about either window, rustling and tapping pleasantly, and Richard was content.

"She does not love me?" Gwyllem cried. "It is well enough. I do not come to her as one merchant to another, since love was never bartered. Listen, Saxon!" He caught up Richard's lute. The strings shrieked beneath Gwyllem's fingers as he fashioned his rude song.

Sang Gwyllem:

> *Love me or love me not, it is enough*
> *That I have loved you, seeing my whole life is*
> *Uplifted and made glad by the glory of Love—*
> *My life that was a scroll all marred and blurred*
> *With tavern-catches, which that pity of his*
> *Erased, and writ instead one perfect word,*
> *O Branwen!*
>
> *I have accorded you incessant praise*
> *And song and service long, O Love, for this,*
> *And always I have dreamed incessantly*
> *Who always dreamed, "When in oncoming days*
> *This man or that shall love you, and at last*
> *This man or that shall win you, it must be*
> *That loving him you will have pity on me*
> *When happiness engenders memory*
> *And long thoughts, nor unkindly, of the past,*
> *O Branwen!"*
>
> *I know not!—ah, I know not, who am sure*
> *That I shall always love you while I live!*
> *And being dead, and with no more to give*

Of song or service?—Love shall yet endure,
And yet retain his last prerogative,
When I lie still, through many centuries,
And dream of you and the exceeding love
I bore you, and am glad dreaming thereof,
And give God thanks therefor, and so find peace,
O Branwen!

"Now, were I to get as tipsy as that," Richard enviously thought, midway in a return to his stolid sheep, "I would simply go to sleep and wake up with a headache. And were I to fall as many fathoms deep in love as this Gwyllem has blundered without any astonishment I would perform—I wonder, now, what miracle?"

For he was, though vaguely, discontent. This Gwyllem was so young, so earnest over every trifle, and above all so unvexed by any rational afterthought; and each desire controlled him as varying winds sport with a fallen leaf, whose frank submission to superior vagaries the boy appeared to emulate. Richard saw that in a fashion Gwyllem was superb. "And heigho!" said Richard, "I am attestedly a greater fool than he, but I begin to weary of a folly so thin-blooded.".

The next morning came a ragged man, riding upon a mule. He claimed to be a tinker. He chatted out an hour with Richard, who perfectly recognized him as Sir Walter Blount; and then this tinker crossed over into England.

And Richard whistled. "Now will my cousin be quite sure, and now will my anxious cousin come to speak with Richard of Bordeaux. And now, by every saint in the calendar! I am as good as King of England."

He sat down beneath a young oak and twisted four or five blades of grass between his fingers what while he meditated. Undoubtedly he would kill Henry of Lancaster with a clear conscience and even with a certain relish, much as one crushes the uglier sort of vermin, but, hand upon heart, he was unable to protest any particularly ardent desire for the scoundrel's death. Thus crudely to demolish the knave's adroit and year-long schemings savored of a tyranny a shade too gross. The spider was venomous, and his destruction laudable; granted, but in crushing him you ruined his web, a miracle of patient malevolence, which, despite yourself, compelled both admiration and envy. True, the process would recrown a certain Richard, but then, as he recalled it, being King was rather tedious. Richard was not now quite sure that he wanted to be King, and in consequence be daily plagued by a host of vexatious and ever-squabbling barons. "I shall miss the little huzzy, too," he thought.

"Heigho!" said Richard, "I shall console myself with purchasing all beautiful things that can be touched and handled. Life is a flimsy vapor which passes and is not any more: presently is Branwen married to this Gwyllem and grown fat and old, and I am remarried to Dame Isabel of France, and am King of England: and a trifle later all four of us will be dead. Pending this deplorable consummation a wise man will endeavor to amuse himself."

Next day he despatched Caradawc to Owain Glyndwyr to bid the latter send the promised implements to Caer Idion. Richard, returning to the hut the same evening, found Alundyne there, alone, and grovelling at the threshold. Her forehead was bloodied when she raised it and through tearless sobs told of the day's happenings. A half-hour since, while she and Branwen were intent upon their milking, Gwyllem had ridden up, somewhat the worse for liquor. Branwen had called him sot, had bidden him go home. "That will I do," said Gwyllem and suddenly caught up the girl. Alundyne sprang for him, and with clenched fist Gwyllem struck her twice full in the face, and laughing, rode away with Branwen.

Richard made no observation. In silence he fetched his horse, and did not pause to saddle it. Quickly he rode to Gwyllem's house, and broke in the door. Against the farther wall stood lithe Branwen fighting silently in a hideous conflict; her breasts and shoulders were naked, where Gwyllem had torn away her garments. He wheedled, laughed, swore, and hiccoughed, turn by turn, but she was silent.

"On guard!" Richard barked. Gwyllem wheeled. His head twisted toward his left shoulder, and one corner of his mouth convulsively snapped upward, so that his teeth were bared. There was a knife at Richard's girdle, which he now unsheathed and flung away. He stepped eagerly toward the snarling Welshman, and with either hand seized the thick and hairy throat. What followed was brutal.

For many minutes Branwen stood with averted face, shuddering. She very dimly heard the sound of Gwyllem's impotent great fists as they beat against the countenance and body of Richard, and the thin splitting vicious noise of torn cloth as Gwyllem clutched at Richard's tunic and tore it many times. Richard uttered no articulate word, and Gwyllem could not. There was entire silence for a heart-beat, and then the fall of something ponderous and limp.

"Come!" Richard said. Through the hut's twilight, glorious in her eyes as Michael fresh from that primal battle, Richard came to her, his face all blood, and lifted her in his arms lest Branwen's skirt be soiled by the demolished thing which sprawled across their path. She never spoke. She could not. In his arms she rode presently, passive, and incuriously content. The horse trod with deliberation. In the east the young moon was taking heart as the darkness thickened about them, and innumerable stars awoke.

Richard was horribly afraid. He it had been, in sober verity it had been Richard of Bordeaux, that some monstrous force had seized, and had lifted, and had curtly utilized as its handiest implement. He had been, and in the moment had known himself to be, the thrown spear as yet in air, about to kill and quite powerless to refrain therefrom. It was a full three minutes before he got the better of his bewilderment and laughed, very softly, lest he disturb this Branwen, who was so near his heart. . .

Next day she came to him at noon, bearing as always the little basket. It contained to-day a napkin, some garlic, a ham, and a small soft cheese; some shalots, salt, nuts, wild apples, lettuce, onions, and mushrooms. "Behold a feast!" said Richard. He noted then that she carried also a blue pitcher filled with thin wine and two cups of oak-bark. She thanked him for last night's performance, and drank a mouthful of wine to his health.

"Decidedly, I shall be sorry to have done with shepherding," said Richard as he ate.

Branwen answered, "I too shall be sorry, lord, when the masquerade is ended." And it seemed to Richard that she sighed, and he was the happier.

But he only shrugged. "I am the wisest person unhanged, since I comprehend my own folly. And so, I think, was once the minstrel of old time that sang: 'Over wild lands and tumbling seas flits Love, at will, and maddens the heart and beguiles the senses of all whom he attacks, whether his quarry be some monster of the ocean or some wild denizen of the forest, or man; for thine, O Love, thine alone is the power to make playthings of us all.'"

"Your bard was wise, no doubt, yet it was not in similar terms that Gwyllem sang of this passion. Lord," she demanded shyly, "how would you sing of love?"

Richard was replete and quite contented with the world. He took up the lute, in full consciousness that his compliance was in large part cenatory. "In courtesy, thus—"

Sang Richard:

> *The gods in honor of fair Branwen's worth*
> *Bore gifts to her—and Jove, Olympus' lord,*
> *Co-rule of Earth and Heaven did accord,*
> *And Venus gave her slender body's girth,*
> *And Mercury the lyre he framed at birth,*
> *And Mars his jewelled and resistless sword,*
> *And wrinkled Plutus all the secret hoard*
> *And immemorial treasure of mid-earth,—*
>
> *And while the puzzled gods were pondering*
> *Which of these goodly gifts the goodliest was,*
> *Dan Cupid came among them carolling*
> *And proffered unto her a looking-glass,*
> *Wherein she gazed and saw the goodliest thing*
> *That Earth had borne, and Heaven might not surpass.*

"Three sounds are rarely heard," said Branwen; "and these are the song of the birds of Rhiannon, an invitation to feast with a miser, and a speech of wisdom from the mouth of a Saxon. The song you have made of courtesy is tinsel. Sing now in verity."

Richard laughed, though he was sensibly nettled and perhaps a shade abashed; and presently he sang again.

Sang Richard:

> *Catullus might have made of words that seek*
> *With rippling sound, in soft recurrent ways,*
> *The perfect song, or in the old dead days*
> *Theocritus have hymned you in glad Greek;*
> *But I am not as they—and dare not speak*
> *Of you unworthily, and dare not praise*
> *Perfection with imperfect roundelays,*
> *And desecrate the prize I dare to seek.*
>
> *I do not woo you, then, by fashioning*
> *Vext similes of you and Guenevere,*
> *And durst not come with agile lips that bring*
> *The sugared periods of a sonneteer,*

JAMES BRANCH CABELL

And bring no more—but just with lips that cling
To yours, and murmur against them, "I love you, dear!"

For Richard had resolved that Branwen should believe him. Tinsel, indeed! then here was yet more tinsel which she must and should receive as gold. He was very angry, because his vanity was hurt, and the pin-prick spurred him to a counterfeit so specious that consciously he gloried in it. He was superb, and she believed him now; there was no questioning the fact, he saw it plainly, and with exultant cruelty; and curt as lightning came the knowledge that she believed the absolute truth.

Richard had taken just two strides, and toward this fair girl. Branwen stayed motionless, her lips a little parted. The affairs of earth and heaven were motionless throughout the moment, attendant, it seemed to him; and his whole life was like a wave, to him, that trembled now at full height, and he was aware of a new world all made of beauty and of pity. Then the lute snapped between his fingers, and Richard shuddered, and his countenance was the face of a man only.

"There is a task," he said, hoarsely—"it is God's work, I think. But I do not know—I only know that you are very beautiful, Branwen," he said, and in the name he found a new and piercing loveliness.

More lately he said: "Go! For I have loved so many women, and, God help me! I know that I have but to wheedle you and you, too, will yield! Yonder is God's work to be done, and within me rages a commonwealth of devils. Child! child!" he cried in agony, "I am, and ever was, a coward, too timid to face life without reserve, and always I laughed because I was afraid to concede that anything is serious!"

For a long while Richard lay at his ease in the lengthening shadows of the afternoon.

"I love her. She thinks me an elderly imbecile with a flat and reedy singing-voice, and she is perfectly right. She has never even entertained the notion of loving me. That is well, for to-morrow, or, it may be, the day after, we must part forever. I would not have the parting make her sorrowful—or not, at least, too unalterably sorrowful. It is very well that Branwen does not love me.

"How should she? I am almost twice her age, an old fellow now, battered and selfish and too indolent to love her—say, as Gwyllem did. I did well to kill that Gwyllem. I am profoundly glad I killed him, and I thoroughly enjoyed doing it; but, after all, the man loved her in his fashion, and to the uttermost reach of his gross nature. I love her in a rather more decorous and acceptable fashion, it is true, but only a half of me loves her; and the other half of me remembers that I am aging, that Caradawc's hut is leaky, that, in fine, bodily comfort is the single luxury of which one never tires. I am a very contemptible creature, the handsome scabbard of a man, precisely as Owain said." This settled, Richard whistled to his dog.

The sun had set, but it was not more than dusk. There were no shadows anywhere as Richard and his sheep went homeward, but on every side the colors of the world were more sombre. Twice his flock roused a covey of partridges which had settled for the night. The screech-owl had come out of his hole, and bats were already blundering about, and the air was more cool. There was as yet but one star in the green and cloudless heaven, and this was very large, like a beacon, and it appeared to him symbolical that he trudged away from it.

Next day the Welshmen came, and now the trap was ready for Henry of Lancaster.

It befell just two days later, about noon, that while Richard idly talked with Branwen a party of soldiers, some fifteen in number, rode down the river's bank from the ford above. Their leader paused, then gave an order. The men drew rein. He cantered forward.

"God give you joy, fair sir," said Richard, when the cavalier was at his elbow.

The new-comer raised his visor. "God give you eternal joy, my fair cousin," he said, "and very soon. Now send away this woman before that happens which must happen."

"You design murder?" Richard said.

"I design my own preservation," King Henry answered, "for while you live my rule is insecure."

"I am sorry," Richard said, "because in part my blood is yours."

Twice he sounded his horn, and everywhere from rustling underwoods arose the half-naked Welshmen. "Your men are one to ten. You are impotent. Now, now we balance our accounts!" cried Richard. "These persons here will first deal with your followers. Then will they conduct you to Glyndwyr, who has long desired to deal with you himself, in privacy, since that Whit Monday when you stabbed his son."

The King began: "In mercy, sire—!" and Richard laughed a little.

"That virtue is not overabundant among us Plantagenets, as both we know. Nay, Fate and Time are merry jesters. See, now, their latest

JAMES BRANCH CABELL

mockery! You the King of England ride to Sycharth to your death, and I the tender of sheep depart into London, without any hindrance, to reign henceforward over all these islands. To-morrow you are worm's-meat; and to-morrow, as aforetime, I am King of England."

Then Branwen gave one sharp, brief cry, and Richard forgot all things saving this girl, and strode to her. He had caught up either of her hard, lithe hands; against his lips he strained them close and very close.

"Branwen—!" he said. His eyes devoured her.

"Yes, King," she answered. "O King of England! O fool that I had been to think you less!"

In a while Richard said: "Now I choose between a peasant wench and England. Now I choose, and, ah, how gladly! O Branwen, help me to be more than King of England!"

Low and very low he spoke, and long and very long he gazed at her and neither seemed to breathe. Of what she thought I cannot tell you; but in Richard there was no power of thought, only a great wonderment. Why, between this woman and aught else there was no choice for him, he knew upon a sudden, and could never be! He was very glad. He loved the tiniest content of the world.

Meanwhile, as from an immense distance, came to this Richard the dogged voice of Henry of Lancaster. "It is of common report in these islands that I have a better right to the throne than you. As much was told our grandfather, King Edward of happy memory, when he educated you and had you acknowledged heir to the crown, but his love was so strong for his son the Prince of Wales that nothing could alter his purpose. And indeed if you had followed even the example of the Black Prince you might still have been our King; but you have always acted so contrarily to his admirable precedents as to occasion the rumor to be generally believed throughout England that you were not, after all, his son—"

Richard had turned impatiently. "For the love of Heaven, truncate your abominable periods. Be off with you. Yonder across that river is the throne of England, which you appear, through some hallucination, to consider a desirable possession. Take it, then; for, praise God! the sword has found its sheath."

The King answered: "I do not ask you to reconsider your dismissal, assuredly—Richard," he cried, a little shaken, "I perceive that until your death you will win contempt and love from every person."

"Ay, for many years I have been the playmate of the world," said Richard; "but to-day I wash my hands, and set about another and more laudable business. I had dreamed certain dreams, indeed—but what had I to do with all this strife between the devil and the tiger? Nay, Glyndwyr will set up Mortimer against you now, and you two must fight it out. I am no more his tool, and no more your enemy, my cousin—Henry," he said with quickening voice, "there was a time when we were boys and played together, and there was no hatred between us, and I regret that time!"

"As God lives, I too regret that time!" the bluff King said. He stared at Richard for a while wherein each understood. "Dear fool," he said, "there is no man in all the world but hates me saving only you." Then the proud King clapped spurs to his proud horse and rode away.

More lately Richard dismissed his wondering marauders. Now were only he and Branwen left, alone and yet a little troubled, since either was afraid of that oncoming moment when their eyes must meet.

So Richard laughed. "Praise God!" he wildly cried, "I am the greatest fool unhanged!"

She answered: "I am the happier. I am the happiest of God's creatures," Branwen said.

And Richard meditated. "Faith of a gentleman!" he declared; "but you are nothing of the sort, and of this fact I happen to be quite certain." Their lips met then and afterward their eyes; and either was too glad for laughter.

THE END OF THE EIGHTH NOVEL

JAMES BRANCH CABELL

IX

The Story of the Navarrese

In the year of grace 1386, upon the feast of Saint Bartholomew (thus Nicolas begins), came to the Spanish coast Messire Peyre de Lesnerac, in a war-ship sumptuously furnished and manned by many persons of dignity and wealth, in order they might suitably escort the Princess Jehane into Brittany, where she was to marry the Duke of that province. There were now rejoicings throughout Navarre, in which the Princess took but a nominal part and young Antoine Riczi none at all.

This Antoine Riczi came to Jehane that August twilight in the hedged garden. "King's daughter!" he sadly greeted her. "Duchess of Brittany! Countess of Rougemont! Lady of Nantes and of Guerrand! of Rais and of Toufon and Guerche!"

"Nay," she answered, "Jehane, whose only title is the Constant Lover." And in the green twilight, lit as yet by one low-hanging star alone, their lips met, as aforetime.

Presently the girl spoke. Her soft mouth was lax and tremulous, and her gray eyes were more brilliant than the star yonder. The boy's arms were about her, so that neither could be quite unhappy; and besides, a sorrow too noble for any bitterness had mastered them, and a vast desire whose aim they could not word, or even apprehend save cloudily.

"Friend," said Jehane, "I have no choice. I must wed with this de Montfort. I think I shall die presently. I have prayed God that I may die before they bring me to the dotard's bed."

Young Riczi held her now in an embrace more brutal. "Mine! mine!" he snarled toward the obscuring heavens.

"Yet it may be I must live. Friend, the man is very old. Is it wicked to think of that? For I cannot but think of his great age."

Then Riczi answered: "My desires—may God forgive me!—have clutched like starving persons at that sorry sustenance. Friend! ah, fair, sweet friend! the man is human and must die, but love, we read, is immortal. I am fain to die, Jehane. But, oh, Jehane! dare you to bid me live?"

"Friend, as you love me, I entreat you live. Friend, I crave of the Eternal Father that if I falter in my love for you I may be denied even the bleak night of ease which Judas knows." The girl did not weep; dry-eyed she winged a perfectly sincere prayer toward incorruptible saints. He was to remember the fact, and through long years.

For even as Riczi left her, yonder behind the yew-hedge a shrill joculatrix sang, in rehearsal for Jehane's bridal feast.

Sang the joculatrix:

> *When the morning broke before us*
> *Came the wayward Three astraying,*
> *Chattering a trivial chorus—*
> *Hoidens that at handball playing*
> *(When they wearied of their playing),*
> *Cast the Ball where now it whirls*
> *Through the coil of clouds unstaying,*
> *For the Fates are merry girls!*

And upon the next day de Lesnerac bore young Jehane from Pampeluna and presently to Saille, where old Jehan the Brave took her to wife. She lived as a queen, but she was a woman of infrequent laughter.

She had Duke Jehan's adoration, and his barons' obeisancy, and his villagers applauded her passage with stentorian shouts. She passed interminable days amid bright curious arrasses and trod listlessly over pavements strewn with flowers. Fiery-hearted jewels she had, and shimmering purple cloths, and much furniture adroitly carven, and many tapestries of Samarcand and Baldach upon which were embroidered, by brown fingers time turned long ago to Asian dust, innumerable asps and deer and phoenixes and dragons and all the motley inhabitants of air and of the thicket: but her memories, too, she had, and for a dreary while she got no comfort because of them. Then ambition quickened.

Young Antoine Riczi likewise nursed his wound as best he might; but about the end of the second year his uncle, the Vicomte de Montbrison—a gaunt man, with preoccupied and troubled eyes—had summoned Antoine into Lyonnois and, after appropriate salutation, had informed the lad that, as the Vicomte's heir, he was to marry the Demoiselle Gerberge de Nerac upon the ensuing Michaelmas.

JAMES BRANCH CABELL

"That I may not do," said Riczi; and since a chronicler that would tempt fortune should never stretch the fabric of his wares too thin, unlike Sir Hengist, I merely tell you these two dwelt together at Montbrison for a decade, and always the Vicomte swore at his nephew and predicted this or that disastrous destination so often as Antoine declined to marry the latest of his uncle's candidates—in whom the Vicomte was of an astonishing fertility.

In the year of grace 1401 came the belated news that Duke Jehan had closed his final day. "You will be leaving me!" the Vicomte growled; "now, in my decrepitude, you will be leaving me! It is abominable, and I shall in all likelihood disinherit you this very night."

"Yet it is necessary," Riczi answered; and, filled with no unhallowed joy, rode not long afterward for Vannes, in Brittany, where the Duchess-Regent held her court. Dame Jehane had within that fortnight put aside her mourning, and sat beneath a green canopy, gold-fringed and powdered with many golden stars, upon the night when he first came to her, and the rising saps of spring were exercising their august and formidable influence. She sat alone, by prearrangement, to one end of the high-ceiled and radiant apartment; midway in the hall her lords and divers ladies were gathered about a saltatrice and a jongleur, who diverted them to the mincing accompaniment of a lute; but Jehane sat apart from these, frail, and splendid with many jewels, and a little sad, and, as ever (he thought), was hers a beauty clarified of its mere substance—the beauty, say, of a moonbeam which penetrates full-grown leaves.

And Antoine Riczi found no power of speech within him at the first. Silent he stood before her for an obvious interval, still as an effigy, while meltingly the jongleur sang.

"Jehane!" said Antoine Riczi, "have you, then, forgotten, O Jehane?"

Nor had the resplendent woman moved at all. It was as though she were some tinted and lavishly adorned statue of barbaric heathenry, and he her postulant; and her large eyes appeared to judge an immeasurable path, beyond him. Now her lips had fluttered somewhat. "The Duchess of Brittany am I," she said, and in the phantom of a voice. "The Countess of Rougemont am I. The Lady of Nantes and of Guerrand! of Rais and of Toufon and Guerche!. . . Jehane is dead."

The man had drawn one audible breath. "You are Jehane, whose only title is the Constant Lover!"

"Friend, the world smirches us," she said half-pleadingly. "I have tasted too deep of wealth and power. Drunk with a deadly wine am I, and ever I thirst—I thirst—"

"Jehane, do you remember that May morning in Pampeluna when first I kissed you, and about us sang many birds? Then as now you wore a gown of green, Jehane."

"Friend, I have swayed kingdoms since."

"Jehane, do you remember that August twilight in Pampeluna when last I kissed you? Then as now you wore a gown of green, Jehane."

"But no such chain as this about my neck," the woman answered, and lifted a huge golden collar garnished with emeralds and sapphires and with many pearls. "Friend, the chain is heavy, yet I lack the will to cast it off. I lack the will, Antoine." And with a sudden roar of mirth her courtiers applauded the evolutions of the saltatrice.

"King's daughter!" said Riczi then; "O perilous merchandise! a god came to me and a sword had pierced his breast. He touched the gold hilt of it and said, 'Take back your weapon.' I answered, 'I do not know you.' 'I am Youth,' he said; 'take back your weapon.'"

"It is true," she responded, "it is lamentably true that after to-night we are as different persons, you and I."

He said: "Jehane, do you not love me any longer? Remember old years and do not break your oath with me, Jehane, since God abhors nothing so much as perfidy. For your own sake, Jehane—ah, no, not for your sake nor for mine, but for the sake of that blithe Jehane, whom, so you tell me, time has slain!"

Once or twice she blinked, as dazzled by a light of intolerable splendor, but otherwise sat rigid. "You have dared, messire, to confront me with the golden-hearted, clean-eyed Navarrese that once was I! and I requite." The austere woman rose. "Messire, you swore to me, long since, an eternal service. I claim my bond. Yonder prim man—gray-bearded, the man in black and silver—is the Earl of Worcester, the King of England's ambassador, in common with whom the wealthy dowager of Brittany has signed a certain contract. Go you, then, with Worcester into England, as my proxy, and in that island, as my proxy, wed the King of England. Messire, your audience is done."

Latterly Riczi said this: "Can you hurt me any more, Jehane?—nay, even in hell they cannot hurt me now. Yet I, at least, keep faith, and in your face I fling faith like a glove—old-fashioned, it may be, but clean—and I will go, Jehane."

Her heart raged. "Poor, glorious fool!" she thought; "had you but the wit even now to use me brutally, even now to drag me from this dais—!" Instead he went from her smilingly, treading through the hall with many affable salutations, while always the jongleur sang.

Sang the jongleur:

> *There is a land the rabble rout*
> *Knows not, whose gates are barred*
> *By Titan twins, named Fear and Doubt,*
> *That mercifully guard*
> *The land we seek—the land so fair!—*
> *And all the fields thereof,*
>
> *Where daffodils grow everywhere*
> *About the Fields of Love—*
> *Knowing that in the Middle-Land*
> *A tiny pool there lies*
> *And serpents from the slimy strand*
> *Lift glittering cold eyes.*
>
> *Now, the parable all may understand,*
> *And surely you know the name o' the land!*
> *Ah, never a guide or ever a chart*
> *May safely lead you about this land,—*
> *The Land of the Human Heart!*

And the following morning, being duly empowered, Antoine Riczi sailed for England in company with the Earl of Worcester, and upon Saint Richard's day the next ensuing was, at Eltham, as proxy of Jehane, married in his own person to the bloat King of England. First had Sire Henry placed the ring on Riczi's finger, and then spoke Antoine Riczi, very loud and clear:

"I, Antoine Riczi—in the name of my worshipful lady, Dame Jehane, the daughter of Messire Charles until lately King of Navarre, the Duchess of Brittany and the Countess of Rougemont—do take you, Sire Henry of Lancaster, King of England and in title of France, and Lord of Ireland, to be my husband; and thereto I, Antoine Riczi, in the spirit of my said lady"—he paused here to regard the gross hulk of masculinity before him, and then smiled very sadly—"in precisely the spirit of my said lady, I plight you my troth."

Afterward the King made him presents of some rich garments of scarlet trimmed with costly furs, and of four silk belts studded with silver and gold, and with valuable clasps, whereof the recipient might well be proud, and Riczi returned to Lyonnois. "Depardieux!" his uncle said; "so you return alone!"

"As Prince Troilus did," said Riczi—"to boast to you of liberal entertainment in the tent of Diomede."

"You are certainly an inveterate fool," the Vicomte considered after a prolonged appraisal of his face, "since there is always a deal of other pink-and-white flesh as yet unmortgaged—Boy with my brother's eyes!" the Vicomte said, and in another voice; "I would that I were God to punish as is fitting! Nay, come home, my lad!—come home!"

So these two abode together at Montbrison for a long time, and in the purlieus of that place hunted and hawked, and made sonnets once in a while, and read aloud from old romances some five days out of the seven. The verses of Riczi were in the year of grace 1410 made public, and not without acclamation; and thereafter the stripling Comte de Charolais, future heir to all Burgundy and a zealous patron of rhyme, was much at Montbrison, and there conceived for Antoine Riczi such admiration as was possible to a very young man only.

In the year of grace 1412 the Vicomte, being then bedridden, died without any disease and of no malady save the inherencies of his age. "I entreat of you, my nephew," he said at last, "that always you use as touchstone the brave deed you did at Eltham. It is necessary a man serve his lady according to her commandments, but you have performed the most absurd and the cruelest task which any woman ever imposed upon her servitor. I laugh at you, and I envy you." Thus he died, about Martinmas.

Now was Antoine Riczi a powerful baron, and got no comfort of his lordship, since in his meditations the King of Darkness, that old incendiary, had added a daily fuel until the ancient sorrow quickened into vaulting flames of wrath and of disgust.

"What now avail my riches?" said the Vicomte. "Nay, how much wealthier was I when I was loved, and was myself an eager lover! I relish no other pleasures than those of love. Love's sot am I, drunk with a deadly wine, poor fool, and ever I thirst. As vapor are all my chattels and my acres, and the more my dominion and my power increase, the more rancorously does my heart sustain its misery, being robbed of that fair merchandise which is the King of England's. To hate her is scant

JAMES BRANCH CABELL

comfort and to despise her none at all, since it follows that I who am unable to forget the wanton am even more to be despised than she. I will go into England and execute what mischief I may against her."

The new Vicomte de Montbrison set forth for Paris, first to do homage for his fief, and secondly to be accredited for some plausible mission into England. But in Paris he got disquieting news. Jehane's husband was dead, and her stepson Henry, the fifth monarch of that name to reign in Britain, had invaded France to support preposterous claims which the man advanced to the very crown of that latter kingdom; and as the earth is altered by the advent of winter was the appearance of France transformed by his coming, and everywhere the nobles were stirred up to arms, the castles were closed, the huddled cities were fortified, and on either hand arose intrenchments.

Thus through this sudden turn was the new Vicomte, the dreamer and the recluse, caught up by the career of events, as a straw is by a torrent, when the French lords marched with their vassals to Harfleur, where they were soundly drubbed by the King of England; as afterward at Agincourt.

But in the year of grace 1417 there was a breathing space for discredited France, and presently the Vicomte de Montbrison was sent into England, as ambassador. He got in London a fruitless audience of King Henry, whose demands were such as rendered a renewal of the war inevitable; and afterward, in the month of April, about the day of Palm Sunday, and within her dower-palace of Havering-Bower, an interview with Queen Jehane.

Nicolas omits, and unaccountably, to mention that during the French wars she had ruled England as Regent, and with marvellous capacity—although this fact, as you will see more lately, is the pivot of his chronicle.

A solitary page ushered the Vicomte whither she sat alone, by prearrangement, in a chamber with painted walls, profusely lighted by the sun, and making pretence to weave a tapestry. When the page had gone she rose and cast aside the shuttle, and then with a glad and wordless cry stumbled toward the Vicomte. "Madame and Queen—!" he coldly said.

A frightened woman, half-distraught, aging now but rather handsome, his judgment saw in her, and no more; all black and shimmering gold his senses found her, and supple like some dangerous and lovely serpent; and with a contained hatred he had discovered, as by the terse illumination of a thunderbolt, that he could never love any woman save the woman whom he most despised.

She said: "I had forgotten. I had remembered only you, Antoine, and Navarre, and the clean-eyed Navarrese—" Now for a little, Jehane paced the gleaming and sun-drenched apartment as a bright leopardess might tread her cage. Then she wheeled. "Friend, I think that God Himself has deigned to avenge you. All misery my reign has been. First Hotspur, then prim Worcester harried us. Came Glyndwyr afterward to prick us with his devil's horns. Followed the dreary years that linked me to the rotting corpse God's leprosy devoured while the poor furtive thing yet moved. All misery, Antoine! And now I live beneath a sword."

"You have earned no more," he said. "You have earned no more, O Jehane! whose only title is the Constant Lover!" He spat it out.

She came uncertainly toward him, as though he had been some not implacable knave with a bludgeon. "For the King hates me," she plaintively said, "and I live beneath a sword. Ever the big fierce-eyed man has hated me, for all his lip-courtesy. And now he lacks the money to pay his troops, and I am the wealthiest person within his realm. I am a woman and alone in a foreign land. So I must wait, and wait, and wait, Antoine, till he devise some trumped-up accusation. Friend, I live as did Saint Damoclus, beneath a sword. Antoine!" she wailed—for now was the pride of Queen Jehane shattered utterly—"within the island am I a prisoner for all that my chains are of gold."

"Yet it was not until o' late," he observed, "that you disliked the metal which is the substance of all crowns."

And now the woman lifted to him a huge golden collar garnished with emeralds and sapphires and with many pearls, and in the sunlight the gems were tawdry things. "Friend, the chain is heavy, and I lack the power to cast it off. The Navarrese we know of wore no such perilous fetters about her neck. Ah, you should have mastered me at Vannes. You could have done so, and very easily. But you only talked—oh, Mary pity us! you only talked!—and I could find only a servant where I had sore need to find a master. Then pity me."

But now came many armed soldiers into the apartment. With spirit Queen Jehane turned to meet them, and you saw that she was of royal blood, for the pride of ill-starred emperors blazed and informed her body as light occupies a lantern. "At last you come for me, messieurs?"

"Whereas," their leader read in answer from a parchment—"whereas the King's stepmother, Queen Jehane, is accused by certain persons

JAMES BRANCH CABELL

of an act of witchcraft that with diabolical and subtle methods wrought privily to destroy the King, the said Dame Jehane is by the King committed (all her attendants being removed), to the custody of Sir John Pelham, who will, at the King's pleasure, confine her within Pevensey Castle, there to be kept under Sir John's control: the lands and other properties of the said Dame Jehane being hereby forfeit to the King, whom God preserve!"

"Harry of Monmouth!" said Jehane—"oh, Harry of Monmouth, could I but come to you, very quietly, and with a knife—!" She shrugged her shoulders, and the gold about her person glittered in the sunlight. "Witchcraft! ohime, one never disproves that. Friend, now are you avenged the more abundantly."

"Young Riczi is avenged," the Vicomte said; "and I came hither desiring vengeance."

She wheeled, a lithe flame (he thought) of splendid fury. "And in the gutter Jehane dares say what Queen Jehane upon the throne might never say. Had I reigned all these years as mistress not of England but of Europe—had nations wheedled me in the place of barons—young Riczi had been avenged, no less. Bah! what do these so-little persons matter? Take now your petty vengeance! drink deep of it! and know that always within my heart the Navarrese has lived to shame me! Know that to-day you despise Jehane, the purchased woman! and that Jehane loves you! and that the love of proud Jehane creeps like a beaten cur toward your feet, and in the sight of common men! and know that Riczi is avenged,—you milliner!"

"Into England I came desiring vengeance—Apples of Sodom! O bitter fruit!" the Vicomte thought; "O fitting harvest of a fool's assiduous husbandry!"

They took her from him: and that afternoon, after long meditation, the Vicomte de Montbrison entreated a fresh and private audience of King Henry, and readily obtained it. "Unhardy is unseely," the Vicomte said at its conclusion. Then the tale tells that the Vicomte returned to France and within this realm assembled all such lords as the abuses of the Queen-Regent Isabeau had more notoriously dissatified.

The Vicomte had upon occasion an invaluable power of speech; and now, so great was the devotion of love's dupe, so heartily, so hastily, did he design to remove the discomforts of Queen Jehane, that now his eloquence was twin to Belial's.

Then presently these lords had sided with King Henry, as had the Vicomte de Montbrison, in open field. Latterly Jehan Sans-Peur was slain at Montereau; and a little later the new Duke of Burgundy, who loved the Vicomte as he loved no other man, had shifted his coat. Afterward fell the poised scale of circumstance, and with an aweful clangor; and now in France clean-hearted persons spoke of the Vicomte de Montbrison as they would of Ganelon or of Iscariot, and in every market-place was King Henry proclaimed as governor of the realm.

Meantime was Queen Jehane conveyed to prison and lodged therein for five years' space. She had the liberty of a tiny garden, high-walled, and of two scantily furnished chambers. The brace of hard-featured females Pelham had provided for the Queen's attendance might speak to her of nothing that occurred without the gates of Pevensey, and she saw no other persons save her confessor, a triple-chinned Dominican; and in fine, had they already lain Jehane within the massive and gilded coffin of a queen the outer world would have made as great a turbulence in her ears.

But in the year of grace 1422, upon the feast of Saint Bartholomew, and about vespers—for thus it wonderfully fell out—one of those grim attendants brought to her the first man, save the fat confessor, whom the Queen had seen within five years. The proud, frail woman looked and what she saw was the common inhabitant of all her dreams.

Said Jehane: "This is ill done. The years have avenged you. Be contented with that knowledge, and, for Heaven's sake, do not endeavor to moralize over the ruin Heaven has made, and justly made, of Queen Jehane, as I perceive you mean to do." She leaned backward in the chair, very coarsely clad in brown, but knowing her countenance to be that of the anemone which naughtily dances above wet earth.

"Friend," the lean-faced man now said, "I do not come with such intent, as my mission will readily attest, nor to any ruin, as your mirror will attest. Nay, madame, I come as the emissary of King Henry, now dying at Vincennes, and with letters to the lords and bishops of his council. Dying, the man restores to you your liberty and your dower-lands, your bed and all your movables, and six gowns of such fashion and such color as you may elect."

Then with hurried speech he told her of five years' events: how within that period King Henry had conquered entire France, and had married the French King's daughter, and had begotten a boy who would presently inherit the united realms of France and England, since in the supreme hour of triumph King Henry had been stricken with a mortal sickness, and now lay dying or perhaps already dead, at Vincennes; and how with his penultimate breath the prostrate conqueror had restored to Queen Jehane all properties and all honors which she formerly enjoyed.

"I shall once more be Regent," the woman said when he had made an end; "Antoine, I shall presently be Regent both of France and of England, since Dame Katharine is but a child." Jehane stood motionless save for the fine hands that plucked the air. "Mistress of Europe! absolute mistress, and with an infant ward! now, may God have mercy on my unfriends, for they will soon perceive great need of it!"

"Yet was mercy ever the prerogative of royal persons," the Vicomte suavely said, "and the Navarrese we know of was both royal and very merciful, O Constant Lover."

The speech was as a whip-lash. Abruptly suspicion kindled in her eyes, as a flame leaps from stick to stick. "Harry of Monmouth feared neither man nor God. It needed more than any death-bed repentance to frighten him into restoral of my liberty." There was a silence. "You, a Frenchman, come as the emissary of King Henry who has devastated France! are there no English lords, then, left alive of all his army?"

The Vicomte de Montbrison said: "There is perhaps no person better fitted to patch up this dishonorable business of your captivity, wherein a clean man might scarcely dare to meddle."

She appraised this, and more lately said with entire irrelevance: "The world has smirched you, somehow. At last you have done something save consider your ill-treatment. I praise God, Antoine, for it brings you nearer."

He told her all. King Henry, it appeared, had dealt with him at Havering in perfect frankness. The King needed money for his wars in France, and failing the seizure of Jehane's enormous wealth, had exhausted every resource. "And France I mean to have," the King said. "Yet the world knows you enjoy the favor of the Comte de Charolais; so get me an alliance with Burgundy against my imbecile brother of France, and Dame Jehane shall repossess her liberty. There you have my price."

"And this price I paid," the Vicomte sternly said, "for 'Unhardy is unseely,' Satan whispered, and I knew that Duke Philippe trusted me. Yea, all Burgundy I marshalled under your stepson's banner, and for three years I fought beneath his loathed banner, until in Troyes we had trapped and slain the last loyal Frenchman. And to-day in France my lands are confiscate, and there is not an honest Frenchman but spits upon my name. All infamy I come to you for this last time, Jehane! as a man already dead I come to you, Jehane, for in France they thirst to murder me, and England has no further need of Montbrison, her blunted and her filthy instrument!"

The woman shuddered. "You have set my thankless service above your life, above your honor even. I find the rhymester glorious and very vile."

"All vile," he answered; "and outworn! King's daughter, I swore to you, long since, eternal service. Of love I freely gave you yonder in Navarre, as yonder at Eltham I crucified my innermost heart for your delectation. Yet I, at least, keep faith, and in your face I fling faith like a glove—outworn, it may be, and, God knows, unclean! Yet I, at least, keep faith! Lands and wealth have I given up for you, O king's daughter, and life itself have I given you, and lifelong service have I given you, and all that I had save honor; and at the last I give you honor, too. Now let the naked fool depart, Jehane, for he has nothing more to give."

She had leaned, while thus he spoke, upon the sill of an open casement. "Indeed, it had been far better," she said, and with averted face, "had we never met. For this love of ours has proven a tyrannous and evil lord. I have had everything, and upon each feast of will and sense the world afforded me this love has swept down, like a harpy—was it not a harpy you called the bird in that old poem of yours?—to rob me of delight. And you have had nothing, for of life he has pilfered you, and he has given you in exchange but dreams, my poor Antoine, and he has led you at the last to infamy. We are as God made us, and—I may not understand why He permits this despotism."

Thereafter, somewhere below, a peasant sang as he passed supperward through the green twilight, lit as yet by one low-hanging star alone.

Sang the peasant:

> *King Jesus hung upon the Cross,*
> *"And have ye sinned?" quo' He,—*
> *"Nay, Dysmas, 'tis no honest loss*
> *When Satan cogs the dice ye toss,*
> *And thou shall sup with Me,—*
> *Sedebis apud angelos,*
> *Quia amavisti!"*

JAMES BRANCH CABELL

> *At Heaven's Gate was Heaven's Queen,*
> *"And have ye sinned?" quo' She,—*
> *"And would I hold him worth a bean*
> *That durst not seek, because unclean,*
> *My cleansing charity?—*
> *Speak thou that wast the Magdalene,*
> *Quia amavisti!"*

"It may be that in some sort the jingle answers me!" then said Jehane; and she began with an odd breathlessness: "Friend, when King Henry dies—and even now he dies—shall I not as Regent possess such power as no woman has ever wielded in Europe? can aught prevent this?"

"Naught," he answered.

"Unless, friend, I were wedded to a Frenchman. Then would the stern English lords never permit that I have any finger in the government." She came to him with conspicuous deliberation and laid one delicate hand upon either shoulder. "Friend, I am aweary of these tinsel splendors. I crave the real kingdom."

Her mouth was tremulous and lax, and her gray eyes were more brilliant than the star yonder. The man's arms were about her, and an ecstasy too noble for any common mirth had mastered them, and a vast desire whose aim they could not word, or even apprehend save cloudily.

And of the man's face I cannot tell you. "King's daughter! mistress of half Europe! I am a beggar, an outcast, as a leper among honorable persons."

But it was as though he had not spoken. "Friend, it was for this I have outlived these garish, fevered years, it was this which made me glad when I was a child and laughed without knowing why. That I might to-day give up this so-great power for love of you, my all-incapable and soiled Antoine, was, as I now know, the end to which the Eternal Father created me. For, look you," she pleaded, "to surrender absolute dominion over half Europe is a sacrifice. Assure me that it is a sacrifice, Antoine! O glorious fool, delude me into the belief that I deny myself in choosing you! Nay, I know it is as nothing beside what you have given up for me, but it is all I have—it is all I have, Antoine!" she wailed in pitiful distress.

He drew a deep and big-lunged breath that seemed to inform his being with an indomitable vigor, and doubt and sorrow went quite away from him. "Love leads us," he said, "and through the sunlight of the world he leads us, and through the filth of it Love leads us, but always in the end, if we but follow without swerving, he leads upward. Yet, O God upon the Cross! Thou that in the article of death didst pardon Dysmas! as what maimed warriors of life, as what bemired travellers in muddied byways, must we presently come to Thee!"

"But hand in hand," she answered; "and He will comprehend."

THE END OF THE NINTH NOVEL

X

The Story of the Fox-Brush

In the year of grace 1417, about Martinmas (thus Nicolas begins), Queen Isabeau fled with her daughter the Lady Katharine to Chartres. There the Queen was met by the Duke of Burgundy, and these two laid their heads together to such good effect that presently they got back into Paris, and in its public places massacred some three thousand Armagnacs. This, however, is a matter which touches history; the root of our concernment is that when the Queen and the Duke rode off to attend to this butcher's business, the Lady Katharine was left behind in the Convent of Saint Scholastica, which then stood upon the outskirts of Chartres, in the bend of the Eure just south of that city. She dwelt a year in this well-ordered place.

There one finds her upon the day of the decollation of Saint John the Baptist, the fine August morning that starts the tale. Katharine the Fair, men called her, with some show of reason. She was very tall, and slim as a rush. Her eyes were large and black, having an extreme lustre, like the gleam of undried ink—a lustre at odd times uncanny. Her abundant hair, too, was black, and to-day doubly sombre by contrast with the gold netting which confined it. Her mouth was scarlet, all curves, and her complexion famous for its brilliancy; only a precisian would have objected that she possessed the Valois nose, long and thin and somewhat unduly overhanging the mouth.

To-day as she came through the orchard, crimson-garbed, she paused with lifted eyebrows. Beyond the orchard wall there was a hodgepodge of noises, among which a nice ear might distinguish the clatter of hoofs, a yelping and scurrying, and a contention of soft bodies, and above all a man's voice commanding the turmoil. She was seventeen, so she climbed into the crotch of an apple-tree and peered over the wall.

He was in rusty brown and not unshabby; but her regard swept over this to his face, and there noted how his eyes were blue winter stars under the tumbled yellow hair, and the flash of his big teeth as he swore between them. He held a dead fox by the brush, which he was cutting off; two hounds, lank and wolfish, were scaling his huge body in frantic attempts to get at the carrion. A horse grazed close at hand.

So for a heart-beat she saw him. Then he flung the tailless body to the hounds, and in the act spied two black eyes peeping through the apple-leaves. He laughed, all mirth to the heels of him. "Mademoiselle, I fear we have disturbed your devotions. But I had not heard that it was a Benedictine custom to rehearse aves in tree-tops." Then, as she leaned forward, both elbows resting more comfortably upon the wall, and thereby disclosing her slim body among the foliage like a crimson flower green-calyxed: "You are not a nun—Blood of God! you are the Princess Katharine!"

The nuns, her present guardians, would have declared the ensuing action horrific, for Katharine smiled frankly at him and demanded how he could be certain of this.

He answered slowly: "I have seen your portrait. Hah, your portrait!" he jeered, head flung back and big teeth glinting in the sunlight. "There is a painter who merits crucifixion."

She considered this indicative of a cruel disposition, but also of a fine taste in the liberal arts. Aloud she stated:

"You are not a Frenchman, messire. I do not understand how you can have seen my portrait."

The man stood for a moment twiddling the fox-brush. "I am a harper, my Princess. I have visited the courts of many kings, though never that of France. I perceive I have been woefully unwise."

This trenched upon insolence—the look of his eyes, indeed, carried it well past the frontier—but she found the statement interesting. Straightway she touched the kernel of those fear-blurred legends whispered about her cradle and now clamant.

"You have, then, seen the King of England?"

"Yes, Highness."

"Is it true that he is an ogre—like Agrapard and Angoulaffre of the Broken Teeth?"

His gaze widened. "I have heard a deal of scandal concerning the man. But never that."

Katharine settled back, luxuriously, in the crotch of the apple-tree. "Tell me about him."

Composedly he sat down upon the grass and began to acquaint her with his knowledge and opinions concerning Henry, the fifth of that name to reign in England. Katharine punctuated his discourse with eager questionings, which are not absolutely to our purpose. In the main this harper thought the man now buffeting France a just king, and, the crown laid aside, he had heard Sire Henry to be sufficiently jovial and even prankish. The harper educed anecdotes. He considered that the King would manifestly take Rouen, which the insatiable man was now besieging. Was the King in treaty for the hand of the Infanta of Aragon? Yes, he undoubtedly was.

Katharine sighed her pity for this ill-starred woman. "And now tell me about yourself."

He was, it appeared, Alain Maquedonnieux, a harper by vocation, and by birth a native of Ireland. Beyond the fact that it was a savage kingdom adjoining Cataia, Katharine knew nothing of Ireland. The harper assured her of anterior misinformation, since the kings of England claimed Ireland as an appanage, though the Irish themselves were of two minds as to the justice of these pretensions; all in all, he considered that Ireland belonged to Saint Patrick, and that the holy man had never accredited a vicar.

"Doubtless, by the advice of God," Alain said: "for I have read in Master Roger de Wendover's Chronicles of how at the dread day of judgment all the Irish are to muster before the high and pious Patrick, as their liege lord and father in the spirit, and by him be conducted into the presence of God; and of how, by virtue of Saint Patrick's request, all the Irish will die seven years to an hour before the second coming of Christ, in order to give the blessed saint sufficient time to marshal his company, which is considerable." Katharine admitted the convenience of this arrangement, as well as the neglect of her education. Alain gazed up at her for a long while, as in reflection, and presently said: "Doubtless the Lady Heleine of Argos also was thus starry-eyed and found in books less diverting reading than in the faces of men." It flooded Katharine's cheeks with a livelier hue, but did not vex her irretrievably; yet, had she chosen to read this man's face, the meaning was plain enough.

I give you the gist of their talk, and that in all conscience is trivial. But it was a day when one entered love's wardship with a splurge, not in more modern fashion venturing forward bit by bit, as though love were so much cold water. So they talked for a long while, with laughter mutually provoked and shared, with divers eloquent and dangerous pauses. The harper squatted upon the ground, the Princess leaned over the wall; but to all intent they sat together upon the loftiest turret of Paradise, and it was a full two hours before Katharine hinted at departure.

Alain rose, approaching the wall. "To-morrow I ride for Milan to take service with Duke Filippo. I had broken my journey these three days past at Chateauneuf yonder, where this fox has been harrying my host's chickens. To-day I went out to slay him, and he led me, his murderer, to the fairest lady earth may boast. Do you not think this fox was a true Christian, my Princess?"

Katharine said: "I lament his destruction. Farewell, Messire Alain! And since chance brought you hither—"

"Destiny brought me hither," Alain affirmed, a mastering hunger in his eyes. "Destiny has been kind; I shall make a prayer to her that she continue so." But when Katharine demanded what this prayer would be, Alain shook his tawny head. "Presently you shall know, Highness, but not now. I return to Chateauneuf on certain necessary businesses; to-morrow I set out at cockcrow for Milan and the Visconti's livery. Farewell!" He mounted and rode away in the golden August sunlight, the hounds frisking about him. The fox-brush was fastened in his hat. Thus Tristran de Leonois may have ridden a-hawking in drowned Cornwall, thus statelily and composedly, Katharine thought, gazing after him. She went to her apartments, singing,

> *El tems amoreus plein de joie,*
> *El tems ou tote riens s'esgaie,*—

and burst into a sudden passion of tears. There were hosts of women-children born every day, she reflected, who were not princesses and therefore compelled to marry ogres; and some of them were beautiful. And minstrels made such an ado over beauty.

Dawn found her in the orchard. She was to remember that it was a cloudy morning, and that mist-tatters trailed from the more distant trees. In the slaty twilight the garden's verdure was lustreless, grass and foliage uniformly sombre save where dewdrops showed like beryls. Nowhere in the orchard was there absolute shadow, nowhere a vista unblurred; but in the east, half-way between horizon and zenith, two belts of coppery light flared against the gray sky like embers swaddled by their ashes. The birds were waking; there were occasional scurryings in tree-tops and outbursts of peevish twittering to attest as much; and presently came a singing, less meritorious than that of many a bird perhaps, but far more grateful to the girl who heard it, heart in mouth. A lute accompanied the song demurely.

Sang Alain:

O Madam Destiny, omnipotent,
Be not too obdurate the while we pray
That this the fleet, sweet time of youth be spent
In laughter as befits a holiday,
From which the evening summons us away,
From which to-morrow wakens us to strife
And toil and grief and wisdom—and to-day
Grudge us not life!

O Madam Destiny, omnipotent,
Why need our elders trouble us at play?
We know that very soon we shall repent
The idle follies of our holiday,
And being old, shall be as wise as they,
But now we are not wise, and lute and fife
Seem sweeter far than wisdom—so to-day
Grudge us not life!

O Madam Destiny, omnipotent,
You have given us youth—and must we cast away
The cup undrained and our one coin unspent
Because our elders' beards and hearts are gray?
They have forgotten that if we delay
Death claps us on the shoulder, and with knife
Or cord or fever mocks the prayer we pray—
"Grudge us not life!"

Madam, recall that in the sun we play
But for an hour, then have the worm for wife,
The tomb for habitation—and to-day
Grudge us not life!

Candor in these matters is best. Katharine scrambled into the crotch of the apple tree. The dew pattered sharply about her, but the Princess was not in a mood to appraise discomfort.

"You came!" this harper said, transfigured; and then again, "You came!"

She breathed, "Yes."

So for a long time they stood looking at each other. She found adoration in his eyes and quailed before it; and in the man's mind not a grimy and mean incident of the past but marshalled to leer at his unworthiness: yet in that primitive garden the first man and woman, meeting, knew no sweeter terror.

It was by the minstrel a familiar earth and the grating speech of earth were earlier regained. "The affair is of the suddenest," Alain observed, and he now swung the lute behind him. He indicated no intention of touching her, though he might easily have done so as he sat there exalted by the height of his horse. "A meteor arrives with more prelude. But Love is an arbitrary lord; desiring my heart, he has seized it, and accordingly I would now brave hell to come to you, and finding you there, esteem hell a pleasure-garden. I have already made my prayer to Destiny that she concede me love, and now of God, our Father and Master, I entreat quick death if I am not to win you. For, God willing, I shall come to you again, though in doing so it were necessary that I split the world like a rotten orange."

"Madness! Oh, brave, sweet madness!" Katharine said. "I am a king's daughter, and you a minstrel."

"Is it madness? Why, then, I think all sensible men are to be commiserated. And indeed I spy in all this some design. Across half the earth I came to you, led by a fox. Heh, God's face!" Alain swore; "the foxes Samson, that old sinewy captain, loosed among the corn of heathenry kindled no disputation such as this fox has set afoot. That was an affair of standing corn and olives spoilt, a bushel or so of disaster; now poised kingdoms topple on the brink of ruin. There will be martial argument shortly if you bid me come again."

"I bid you come," said Katharine; and after they had stared at each other for a long while, he rode away in silence. It was through a dank, tear-flawed world that she stumbled conventward, while out of the east the sun came bathed in mists, a watery sun no brighter than a silver coin.

And for a month the world seemed no less dreary, but about Michaelmas the Queen-Regent sent for her. At the Hotel de Saint-Pol matters were much the same. Her mother Katharine found in foul-mouthed rage over the failure of a third attempt to poison the Dauphin of Vienne, as Isabeau had previously poisoned her two elder sons; I might here trace out a curious similitude between the Valois and that dragon-spawned race which Jason very anciently slew at Colchis, since the world was never at peace so long as any two of them existed: but King Charles greeted his daughter with ampler deference, esteeming her Presbyter John's wife, the tyrant of Ethiopia. However, ingenuity had just suggested card-playing for his amusement, and he paid little attention nowadays to any one save his opponent.

So the French King chirped his senile jests over the card-table, while the King of England was besieging the French city of Rouen sedulously and without mercy. In late autumn an armament from Ireland joined Henry's forces. The Irish fought naked, it was said, with long knives. Katharine heard discreditable tales of these Irish, and reflected how gross are the exaggerations of rumor.

In the year of grace 1419, in January, the burgesses of Rouen, having consumed their horses, and finding frogs and rats unpalatable, yielded the town. It was the Queen-Regent who brought the news to Katharine.

"God is asleep," the Queen said; "and while He nods, the Butcher of Agincourt has stolen our good city of Rouen." She sat down and breathed heavily. "Never was poor woman so pestered as I! The puddings to-day were quite uneatable, and on Sunday the Englishman entered Rouen in great splendor, attended by his chief nobles; but the Butcher rode alone, and before him went a page carrying a fox-brush on the point of his lance. I put it to you, is that the contrivance of a sane man? Euh! euh!" Dame Isabeau squealed on a sudden; "you are bruising me."

Katharine had gripped her by the shoulder. "The King of England—a tall, fair man? with big teeth? a tiny wen upon his neck—here—and with his left cheek scarred? with blue eyes, very bright, bright as tapers?" She poured out her questions in a torrent, and awaited the answer, seeming not to breathe at all.

"I believe so," the Queen said.

"O God!" said Katharine.

"Ay, our only hope now. And may God show him no more mercy than he has shown us!" the good lady desired, with fervor. "The hog, having won our Normandy, is now advancing on Paris itself. He repudiated the Aragonish alliance last August; and until last August he was content with Normandy, they tell us, but now he swears to win all France. The man is a madman, and Scythian Tamburlaine was more lenient. And I do not believe that in all France there is a cook who understands his business." She went away whimpering and proceeded to get tipsy.

The Princess remained quite still, as Dame Isabeau had left her; you may see a hare crouch so at sight of the hounds. Finally the girl spoke aloud. "Until last August!" Katharine said. "Until last August! *Poised kingdoms topple on the brink of ruin, now that you bid me come to you again*. And I bade him come!" Presently she went into her oratory and began to pray.

In the midst of her invocation she wailed: "Fool, fool! How could I have thought him less than a king!"

You are to imagine her breast thus adrum with remorse and hatred of herself, what time town by town fell before the invader like card-houses. Every rumor of defeat—and they were many—was her arraignment; impotently she cowered at God's knees, knowing herself a murderess, whose infamy was still afoot, outpacing her prayers, whose victims were battalions. Tarpeia and Pisidice and Rahab were her sisters; she hungered in her abasement for Judith's nobler guilt.

In May he came to her. A truce was patched up and French and English met amicably in a great plain near Meulan. A square space was staked out and on three sides boarded in, the fourth side being the river Seine. This enclosure the Queen-Regent, Jehan of Burgundy, and Katharine entered from the French side. Simultaneously the English King appeared, accompanied by his brothers the Dukes of Clarence and Gloucester, and followed by the Earl of Warwick. Katharine raised her eyes with I know not what lingering hope; it was he, a young Zeus now, triumphant and uneager. In his helmet in place of a plume he wore a fox-brush spangled with jewels.

These six entered the tent pitched for the conference—the hanging of blue velvet embroidered with fleurs-de-lys of gold blurred before the girl's eyes, and till death the device sickened her—and there the Earl of Warwick embarked upon a sea of rhetoric. His French was indifferent, his periods interminable, and his demands exorbitant; in brief, the King of England wanted Katharine and most of France, with a reversion at the French King's death of the entire kingdom. Meanwhile Sire Henry sat in silence, his eyes glowing.

"I have come," he said, under cover of Warwick's oratory—"I have come again, my lady."

Katharine's gaze flickered over him. "Liar!" she said, very softly. "Has God no thunder in His armory that this vile thief should go unblasted? Would you filch love as well as kingdoms?"

His ruddy face went white. "I love you, Katharine."

"Yes," she answered, "for I am your pretext. I can well believe, messire, that you love your pretext for theft and murder."

Neither spoke after this, and presently the Earl of Warwick having come to his peroration, the matter was adjourned till the next day. The party separated. It was not long before Katharine had informed her mother that, God willing, she would never again look upon the King of England's face uncoffined. Isabeau found her a madwoman. The girl swept opposition before her with gusts of demoniacal fury, wept, shrieked, tore at her hair, and eventually fell into a sort of epileptic seizure; between rage and terror she became a horrid, frenzied beast. I do not dwell upon this, for it is not a condition in which the comeliest maid shows to advantage. But, for the Valois, insanity always lurked at the next corner, expectant, and they knew it; to save the girl's reason the Queen was forced to break off all discussion of the match. Accordingly, the Duke of Burgundy went next day to the conference alone. Jehan began with "ifs," and over these flimsy barriers Henry, already maddened by Katharine's scorn, presently vaulted to a towering fury.

"Fair cousin," the King said, after a deal of vehement bickering, "we wish you to know that we will have the daughter of your King, and that we will drive both him and you out of this kingdom."

The Duke answered, not without spirit: "Sire, you are pleased to say so; but before you have succeeded in ousting my lord and me from this realm, I am of the opinion that you will be very heartily tired."

At this the King turned on his heel; over his shoulder he flung: "I am tireless; also, I am agile as a fox in the pursuit of my desires. Say that to your Princess." Then he went away in a rage.

It had seemed an approvable business to win love incognito, according to the example of many ancient emperors, but in practice he had tripped over an ugly outgrowth from the legendary custom. The girl hated him, there was no doubt about it; and it was equally certain he loved her. Particularly caustic was the reflection that a twitch of his finger would get him Katharine as his wife, for in secret negotiation the Queen-Regent was soon trying to bring this about; yes, he could get the girl's body by a couple of pen-strokes; but, God's face! what he wanted was to rouse the look her eyes had borne in Chartres orchard that tranquil morning, and this one could not readily secure by fiddling with seals and parchments. You see his position: he loved the Princess too utterly to take her on lip-consent, and this marriage was now his one possible excuse for ceasing from victorious warfare. So he blustered, and the fighting recommenced; and he slew in a despairing rage, knowing that by every movement of his arm he became to her so much the more detestable.

He stripped the realm of provinces as you peel the layers from an onion. By the May of the year of grace 1420 France was, and knew herself to be, not beaten but demolished. Only a fag-end of the French army lay entrenched at Troyes, where the court awaited Henry's decision as to the morrow's action. If he chose to destroy them root and branch, he could; and they knew such mercy as was in the man to be quite untarnished by previous usage. He drew up a small force before the city and made no overtures toward either peace or throat-cutting.

This was the posture of affairs on the evening of the Sunday after Ascension day, when Katharine sat at cards with her father in his apartments at the Hotel de Ville. The King was pursing his lips over an alternative play, when there came the voice of one singing below in the courtyard.

Sang the voice:

> *I get no joy of my life*
> *That have weighed the world—and it was*
> *Abundant with folly, and rife*
> *With sorrows brittle as glass,*
> *And with joys that flicker and pass*
> *As dreams through a fevered head,*
> *And like the dripping of rain*
> *In gardens naked and dead*
> *Is the obdurate thin refrain*
> *Of our youth which is presently dead.*
>
> *And she whom alone I have loved*
> *Looks ever with loathing on me,*
> *As one she hath seen disproved*
> *And stained with such smirches as be*
> *Not ever cleansed utterly,*
> *And is loth to remember the days*
> *When Destiny fixed her name*
> *As the theme and the goal of my praise,*

And my love engenders shame,
And I stain what I strive for and praise.

O love, most perfect of all,
Just to have known you is well!
And it heartens me now to recall
That just to have known you is well,
And naught else is desirable
Save only to do as you willed
And to love you my whole life long—
But this heart in me is filled
With hunger cruel and strong,
And with hunger unfulfilled.

O Love, that art stronger than we,
Albeit not lightly stilled,
Thou art less cruel than she.

Malise came hastily into the room, and, without speaking, laid a fox-brush before the Princess.

Katharine twirled it in her hand, staring at the card-littered table. "So you are in his pay, Malise? I am sorry. But you know that your employer is master here. Who am I to forbid him entrance?" The girl went away silently, abashed, and the Princess sat quite still, tapping the brush against the table.

"They do not want me to sign another treaty, do they?" her father asked timidly. "It appears to me they are always signing treaties, and I cannot see that any good comes of it. And I would have won the last game, Katharine, if Malise had not interrupted us. You know I would have won."

"Yes, father, you would have won. Oh, he must not see you!" Katharine cried, a great tide of love mounting in her breast, the love that draws a mother fiercely to shield her backward boy. "Father, will you not go into your chamber? I have a new book for you, father—all pictures, dear. Come—" She was coaxing him when Henry appeared in the doorway.

"But I do not wish to look at pictures," Charles said, peevishly; "I wish to play cards. You are an ungrateful daughter, Katharine. You are never willing to amuse me." He sat down with a whimper and began to pinch at his dribbling lips.

Katharine had moved a little toward the door. Her face was white. "Now welcome, sire!" she said. "Welcome, O great conqueror, who in your hour of triumph can find no nobler recreation than to shame a maid with her past folly! It was valorously done, sire. See, father; here is the King of England come to observe how low we sit that yesterday were lords of France."

"The King of England!" echoed Charles, and rose now to his feet. "I thought we were at war with him. But my memory is treacherous. You perceive, brother of England, I am planning a new mouse-trap, and my mind is somewhat preempted. I recall now you are in treaty for my daughter's hand. Katharine is a good girl, messire, but I suppose—" He paused, as if to regard and hear some insensible counsellor, and then briskly resumed: "Yes, I suppose policy demands that she should marry you. We trammelled kings can never go free of policy—ey, my compere of England? No; it was through policy I wedded her mother; and we have been very unhappy, Isabeau and I. A word in your ear, son-in-law: Madame Isabeau's soul formerly inhabited a sow, as Pythagoras teaches, and when our Saviour cast it out at Gadara, the influence of the moon drew it hither."

Henry did not say anything. Always his calm blue eyes appraised Dame Katharine.

"Oho, these Latinists cannot hoodwink me, you observe, though by ordinary it chimes with my humor to appear content. Policy again, messire: for once roused, I am terrible. To-day in the great hall-window, under the bleeding feet of Lazarus, I slew ten flies—very black they were, the black shrivelled souls of parricides—and afterward I wept for it. I often weep; the Mediterranean hath its sources in my eyes, for my daughter cheats at cards. Cheats, sir!—and I her father!" The incessant peering, the stealthy cunning with which Charles whispered this, the confidence with which he clung to his destroyer's hand, was that of a conspiring child.

"Come, father," Katharine said. "Come away to bed, dear."

"Hideous basilisk!" he spat at her; "dare you rebel against me? Am I not King of France, and is it not blasphemy a King of France should be thus mocked? Frail moths that flutter about my splendor." He shrieked, in an unheralded frenzy, "beware of me, beware! for I am omnipotent! I am King of France, God's regent. At my command the winds go about the earth, and nightly the stars are kindled for my recreation. Perhaps I am mightier than God, but I do not remember now. The

JAMES BRANCH CABELL

reason is written down and lies somewhere under a bench. Now I sail for England. Eia! eia! I go to ravage England, terrible and merciless. But I must have my mouse-traps, Goodman Devil, for in England the cats o' the middle-sea wait unfed." He went out of the room, giggling, and in the corridor began to sing:

> *Adieu de fois plus de cent mile!*
> *Aillors vois oir l'Evangile,*
> *Car chi fors mentir on ne sait. . .*

All this while Henry remained immovable, his eyes fixed upon Katharine. Thus (she meditated) he stood among Frenchmen; he was the boulder, and they the waters that babbled and fretted about him. But she turned and met his gaze squarely.

"And that," she said, "is the king whom you have conquered! Is it not a notable conquest to overcome so sapient a king? to pilfer renown from an idiot? There are pickpockets in Troyes, rogues doubly damned, who would scorn the action. Now shall I fetch my mother, sire? the commander of that great army which you overcame? As the hour is late she is by this tipsy, but she will come. Or perhaps she is with some paid lover, but if this conqueror, this second Alexander, wills it she will come. O God!" the girl wailed, on a sudden; "O just and all-seeing God! are not we of Valois so contemptible that in conquering us it is the victor who is shamed?"

"Flower o' the marsh!" he said, and his big voice pulsed with many tender cadences—"flower o' the marsh! it is not the King of England who now comes to you, but Alain the harper. Henry Plantagenet God has led hither by the hand to punish the sins of this realm and to reign in it like a true king. Henry Plantagenet will cast out the Valois from the throne they have defiled, as Darius Belshazzar, for such is the desire and the intent of God. But to you comes Alain the harper, not as a conqueror but as a suppliant—Alain who has loved you whole-heartedly these two years past and who now kneels before you entreating grace."

Katharine looked down into his countenance, for to his speech he had fitted action. Suddenly and for the first time she understood that he believed France his by a divine favor and Heaven's peculiar intervention. He thought himself God's factor, not His rebel. He was rather stupid, this huge handsome boy; and realizing it, her hand went to his shoulder, half maternally.

"It is nobly done, sire. I know that you must wed me to uphold your claim to France, for otherwise in the world's eyes you are shamed. You sell, and I with my body purchase, peace for France. There is no need of a lover's posture when hucksters meet."

"So changed!" he said, and he was silent for an interval, still kneeling. Then he began: "You force me to point out that I no longer need a pretext to hold France. France lies before me prostrate. By God's singular grace I reign in this fair kingdom, mine by right of conquest, and an alliance with the house of Valois will neither make nor mar me." She was unable to deny this, unpalatable as was the fact. "But I love you, and therefore as man wooes woman I sue to you. Do you not understand that there can be between us no question of expediency? Katharine, in Chartres orchard there met a man and a maid we know of; now in Troyes they meet again—not as princess and king, but as man and maid, the wooer and the wooed. Once I touched your heart, I think. And now in all the world there is one thing I covet—to gain for the poor king some portion of that love you would have squandered on the harper." His hand closed upon hers.

At his touch the girl's composure vanished. "My lord, you woo too timidly for one who comes with many loud-voiced advocates. I am daughter to the King of France, and next to my soul's salvation I esteem France's welfare. Can I, then, fail to love the King of England, who chooses the blood of my countrymen as a judicious garb to come a-wooing in? How else, since you have ravaged my native land, since you have besmirched the name I bear, since yonder afield every wound in my dead and yet unburied Frenchmen is to me a mouth which shrieks your infamy?"

He rose. "And yet, for all that, you love me."

She could not find words with which to answer him at the first effort, but presently she said, quite simply, "To see you lying in your coffin I would willingly give up my hope of heaven, for heaven can afford no sight more desirable."

"You loved Alain."

"I loved the husk of a man. You can never comprehend how utterly I loved him."

Now I have to record of this great king a piece of magnanimity which bears the impress of more ancient times. "That you love me is indisputable," he said, "and this I propose to demonstrate. You will observe that I am quite unarmed save for this dagger, which I now throw

JAMES BRANCH CABELL

out of the window—" with the word it jangled in the courtyard below. "I am in Troyes alone among some thousand Frenchmen, any one of whom would willingly give his life for the privilege of taking mine. You have but to sound the gong beside you, and in a few moments I shall be a dead man. Strike, then! for with me dies the English power in France. Strike, Katharine! if you see in me but the King of England."

She was rigid; and his heart leapt when he saw it was because of terror.

"You came alone! You dared!"

He answered, with a wonderful smile, "Proud spirit! how else might I conquer you?"

"You have not conquered!" Katharine lifted the baton beside the gong, poising it. God had granted her prayer—to save France. Now might the past and the ignominy of the past be merged in Judith's nobler guilt. But I must tell you that in the supreme hour, Destiny at her beck, her main desire was to slap the man for his childishness. Oh, he had no right thus to besot himself with adoration! This dejection at her feet of his high destiny awed her, and pricked her, too, with her inability to understand him. Angrily she flung away the baton. "Go! ah, go!" she cried, as one strangling. "There has been enough of bloodshed, and I must spare you, loathing you as I do, for I cannot with my own hand murder you."

But the King was a kindly tyrant, crushing independence from his associates as lesser folk squeeze water from a sponge. "I cannot go thus. Acknowledge me to be Alain, the man you love, or else strike upon the gong."

"You are cruel!" she wailed, in her torture.

"Yes, I am cruel."

Katharine raised straining arms above her head in a hard gesture of despair. "You have conquered. You know that I love you. Oh, if I could find words to voice my shame, to shriek it in your face, I could better endure it! For I love you. Body and heart and soul I am your slave. Mine is the agony, for I love you! and presently I shall stand quite still and see little Frenchmen scramble about you as hounds leap about a stag, and afterward kill you. And after that I shall live! I preserve France, but after I have slain you, Henry, I must live. Mine is the agony, the enduring agony." She stayed motionless for an interval. "God, God! let me not fail!" Katharine breathed; and then: "O fair sweet friend, I am about to commit a vile action, but it is for the sake of France that I love next to God. As Judith gave her body to Holofernes, I crucify my heart for France's welfare." Very calmly she struck upon the gong.

If she could have found any reproach in his eyes during the ensuing silence, she could have borne it; but there was only love. And with all that, he smiled as one knowing the upshot of the matter.

A man-at-arms came into the room. "Germain—" Katharine said, and then again, "Germain—" She gave a swallowing motion and was silent. When she spoke it was with crisp distinctness. "Germain, fetch a harp. Messire Alain here is about to play for me."

At the man's departure she said: "I am very pitiably weak. Need you have dragged my soul, too, in the dust? God heard my prayer, and you have forced me to deny His favor, as Peter denied Christ. My dear, be very kind to me, for I come to you naked of honor." She fell at the King's feet, embracing his knees. "My master, be very kind to me, for there remains only your love."

He raised her to his breast. "Love is enough," he said.

Next day the English entered Troyes and in the cathedral church these two were betrothed. Henry was there magnificent in a curious suit of burnished armor; in place of his helmet-plume he wore a fox-brush ornamented with jewels, which unusual ornament afforded great matter of remark among the busy bodies of both armies.

THE END OF THE TENTH NOVEL

The Epilogue

A son Livret

Intrepidly depart, my little book, into the presence of that most illustrious lady who bade me compile you. Bow down before her judgment patiently. And if her sentence be that of death I counsel you to grieve not at what cannot be avoided.

But, if by any miracle that glorious, strong fortress of the weak consider it advisable, pass thence to every man who may desire to purchase you, and live out your little hour among these very credulous persons; and at your appointed season die and be forgotten. For thus only may you share your betters' fate, and be at one with those famed comedies of Greek Menander and all the poignant songs of Sappho. *Et quid Pandoniae*—thus, little book, I charge you poultice your more-merited oblivion—*quid Pandoniae restat nisi nomen Athenae*?

Yet even in your brief existence you may chance to meet with those who will affirm that the stories you narrate are not verily true and erroneously protest too many assertions which are only fables. To these you will reply that I, your maker, was in my youth the quite unworthy servant of the most high and noble lady, Dame Jehane, and in this period, at and about her house of Havering-Bower, conversed in my own person with Dame Katharine, then happily remarried to a private gentleman of Wales; and so obtained the matter of the ninth story and of the tenth authentically. You will say also that Messire de Montbrison afforded me the main matter of the sixth and seventh stories; and that, moreover, I once journeyed to Caer Idion and talked for some two hours with Richard Holland (whom I found a very old and garrulous and cheery person), and got of him the matter of the eighth tale in this dizain, together with much information as concerns the sixth and the seventh. And you will add that the matter of the fourth and fifth tales was in every detail related to me by my most illustrious mistress, Madame Isabella of Portugal, who had it from her mother, an equally veracious and immaculate lady, and one that was in youth Dame Philippa's most dear associate. For the rest you must admit, unwillingly, the first three stories in this book to be a thought less solidly confirmed; although (as you will say) even in these I have not ever deviated from what was at odd times narrated to me by the aforementioned persons, and have always endeavored honestly to piece together that which they told me.

Also, my little book, you will encounter more malignant people who will jeer at you, and say that you and I have cheated them of your purchase-money. To these you will reply, with Plutarch, *Non mi aurum posco, nec mi pretium*. Secondly you will say that, of necessity, the tailor cuts the coat according to his cloth; and that he cannot undertake to robe an Ephialtes or a towering Orion suitably when the resources of his shop amount at most to three scant yards of cambric. Indeed had I the power to make you better, my little book, I would have done it. A good conscience is a continual feast, and I summon all heaven to be my witness that had I been Homer you had awed the world, another Iliad. I lament the improbability of your doing this as heartily as any person living; yet Heaven willed it; and it is in consequence to Heaven these same cavillers should now complain if they insist upon considering themselves to be aggrieved.

So to such impious people do you make no answer at all, unless indeed you should elect to answer them by repetition of this trivial song which I now make for you, my little book, at your departure from me. And the song runs in this fashion:

> *Depart, depart, my book! and live and die*
> *Dependent on the idle fantasy*
> *Of men who cannot view you, quite, as I.*
>
> *For I am fond, and willingly mistake*
> *My book to be the book I meant to make,*
> *And cannot judge you, for that phantom's sake.*
>
> *Yet pardon me if I have wrought too ill*
> *In making you, that never spared the will*
> *To shape you perfectly, and lacked the skill.*
>
> *Ah, had I but the power, my book, then I*
> *Had wrought in you some wizardry so high*
> *That no man but had listened. . . !*
>
> *They pass by,*
> *And shrug—as we, who know that unto us*

It has been granted never to fare thus,
And never to be strong and glorious.

Is it denied me to perpetuate
What so much loving labor did create?—
I hear Oblivion tap upon the gate,
And acquiesce, not all disconsolate.

For I have got such recompense
Of that high-hearted excellence
Which the contented craftsman knows,
Alone, that to loved labor goes,
And daily doth the work he chose,
And counts all else impertinence!

EXPLICIT DECAS REGINARUM

A Note About the Author

James Branch Cabell (1879–1958) was an American writer of escapist and fantasy fiction. Born into a wealthy family in the state of Virginia, Cabell attended the College of William and Mary, where he graduated in 1898 following a brief personal scandal. His first stories began to be published, launching a productive decade in which Cabell's worked appeared in both *Harper's Monthly Magazine* and *The Saturday Evening Post*. Over the next forty years, Cabell would go on to publish fifty-two books, many of them novels and short-story collections. A friend, colleague, and inspiration for such writers as Ellen Glasgow, H.L. Mencken, Sinclair Lewis, and Theodore Dreiser, James Branch Cabell is remembered as an iconoclastic pioneer of fantasy literature.

A Note from the Publisher

Spanning many genres, from non-fiction essays to literature classics to children's books and lyric poetry, Mint Edition books showcase the master works of our time in a modern new package. The text is freshly typeset, is clean and easy to read, and features a new note about the author in each volume. Many books also include exclusive new introductory material. Every book boasts a striking new cover, which makes it as appropriate for collecting as it is for gift giving. Mint Edition books are only printed when a reader orders them, so natural resources are not wasted. We're proud that our books are never manufactured in excess and exist only in the exact quantity they need to be read and enjoyed.

bookfinity™

Discover more of your favorite classics with Bookfinity™.

- Track your reading with custom book lists.
- Get great book recommendations for your personalized Reader Type.
- Add reviews for your favorite books.
- AND MUCH MORE!

Visit **bookfinity.com** and take the fun Reader Type quiz to get started.

Enjoy our classic and modern companion pairings!

Classic & Modern

9 781513 267609